The
CHRONICLES
of The
WHITE HORSE

For S K

The
CHRONICLES
of The
WHITE HORSE

Peter Please

The Findhorn Press

ISBN 0 905249 57 7
First published 1982
Copyright © Peter Please 1982
Illustrations copyright © Caroline Waterlow 1982

Set in 11/11½ point Garamond
Printed and published by The Findhorn Press,
Moray, Scotland

The thirteen songs in this book have been recorded
by Peter Please and a group of English and Irish
musicians, played on instruments as varied as the
hammered dulcimer, Irish pipes, mandolin and accordion,
for release in the summer of 1982. For further details
please write to the publishers.

Cover design by Caroline Waterlow and John Button

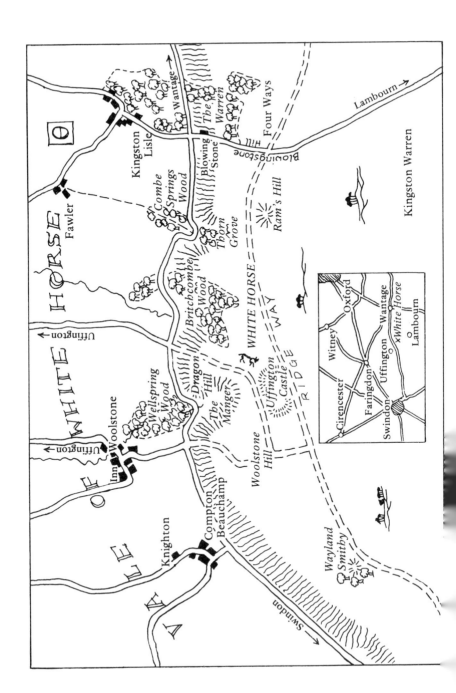

Chapter One

When I was nine I made a promise. I'll keep it now I'm eighty. I'll keep it here among these trees, I'll keep it in this valley. There is no-one to tell it to now. My brothers and sisters have gone, along with the few friends I ever made. I never married. Perhaps the pity, perhaps the pity not. I might have stayed in one place. I might have seen the sun rise on Ram's Hill each day. You may wonder who I am. I wonder who you are. I will tell you about myself.

My name is Fellman Clack. I left my father's farm as the youngest son always did. That was in the greensand beyond White Horse Hill in the county of Berkshire. I left in my twentieth year, with four golden guineas my father gave me. I still have one hidden in this raincoat, an army issue nearly as old as my wanderings. I am saving the guinea for my funeral. Whoever finds these papers, please make sure my ashes are scattered in this valley with a little ceremony. It is my last wish. The guinea is yours and you will find it sewn into the left-hand lapel.

My coat is my oldest friend. It shelters me from the rain, it shields me from the frost. I carry my food in the side pockets. I keep my papers, including these, in the lining. The possessions of a lifetime I keep in a small inside pocket. I lie on my coat on summer nights. I sleep in it on winter nights when I can't find a barn or I am too far from a shilling hostel. I lost the buttons long ago, but the plastic binder-cord is just as good around the middle. In this coat I have been making journeys all my life. I have been a tinker, a soldier and a shoemaker. I never went to sea. I never returned to the land. They know my face in every village along the greensand, from Wantage to Avebury; and in all the villages of the upper Thames, from Cricklade to Oxford City. There will be no more journeyings. Who will remember me then?

Isn't it strange how I return like the salmon to the places of my childhood. These thorn trees. These blessed thorn trees! They are still here. The sarsen stone, too. When I was four I imagined these hills to be the farthest place away in the world, where there were no people or tracks. It was where the wind came from which tasted sweet. No-one went there except for sheep and shepherds. It has hardly changed. The sheep are still there, but there are no shepherds.

Perhaps it was because I was on the small side, a pint in a half pot my father used to say, that my father weaned me from the land at a small age. He made me count the milk yields or do other simple counting jobs. He made sure I went to school, not like my two elder brothers. I think he had me in mind as a clerk, perhaps to a cornmerchant in Faringdon. He was more farsighted than I. He knew the farmworkers were lingering on the land like dodos.

I still have memories of him in warm, buttery colours, and his curly hair which I inherited and have to this day. I always associate my father with rooks, for they both return-ed home from the fields at the same time, my father to our red-bricked thatched cottage, the rooks to the elms at nearby

Fawler. Even today, if I have the chance, I make my camp at rookeries so I can sit at dusk listening to their cries and those faraway memories. I once returned to the farm and found ghosts instead of trees, and a huge field with barbed-wire fences. Those days have gone forever. Who can remember the dust clouds which followed the drovers to Isley fair? Who remembers the dancing bear, the horse-ploughing teams, the women in the fields? Time. Time. It's all gone with time. It walked with the horse then, now it flies with the jets.

I like being on high places, not exposed on the top, but lower down in a gulley, ditch or valley so I am sheltered and concealed. Thorngrove is like that, hidden from the main road at the bottom of the Downs by a bluff formed by two other valleys. It is a place you discover by accident as I did over seventy years ago when I ran stumbling into this valley. I call it Thorngrove, for there is an old grove of thorns at the top, below the crown of Ram's Hill. The grove is a little miracle for normally the sheep cut down everything that grows through the grass. But not so Thorngrove. The trees are still as old and as vital as I remember them from my childhood. In a way, I call this place my home.

At the age of nine I was a child with one passion. I loved collecting animals. I had such a big zoo that I charged my friends a farthing to visit. The slow-worms I found in the

village graveyard, the bull toad in a sand bucket. The big orange newts came from Kingstone Lisle pond, the hearth crickets from the cottage, as well as many other crawly things from the hedgerows. I kept my zoo at the bottom of the kitchen garden in cages, buckets, old sinks, and, when I had too many creatures, I brought them into my bedroom. It was my secret world, and when I was not doing homework or chores, I was out hunting and adding to my collection.

This story, in a strange sort of way, is about my zoo, but it is also about a friend. I fear many things will be left unsaid, for who can recover the spilled water from the well? My eyes are failing but I see the colour of those days more clearly than the moss on this sarsen stone. This story is about the nameless ones of the trees and hills, the little things in hedgerows and at the bottom of ditches. All blessings to them! When the dew has fallen and before first light, I sit on this stone and listen for the sound they make. I call it the sound of the star breaking. It is getting harder and harder to hear it for the hills are becoming silent.

If I should lose my way or mix things up, then I am responsible. If there is poetry, laughter, half-hidden things; if it seems crazy at times, then all I can say is that I did not choose it. It happened that way. Oh, if my legs were strong! I would run on the sweet horse gallops, count the larks above White Horse Hill. I would get thyme in my hair again and pick the goosegrass from my shorts.

> I wish I was on White Horse Hill
> At the breaking of my day;
> Along the sweet horse gallops I'd run,
> And in the stars I'd play.
>> Where daisies fall, nightingales call
>> Little owls to play.
>> Oh I wish I was on White Horse Hill
>> At the breaking of my day.
>
> Come crows come sheep come chalk hedgerows,
> I'd fly the big green hill.
> Come nights come snow come stars' haloes,
> I'd follow the greensand trail.
>> Where daisies fall, nightingales call
>> Little owls to play.
>> Oh I wish I was on White Horse Hill
>> At the breaking of my day.
>
> The horse the pack the moon the track,
> All travel the north wind road.

The Thames it flows, the man down he goes
Along his winter road,
Far down his winter road.
    Where daisies fall, nightingales call
    Little owls to play.
    Oh I wish I was on White Horse Hill
    At the breaking of my day.

As I said, when I was nine I made a promise and I'll keep
it now I'm eighty. This is for my friend Ben, a detective in
little things, and the journey we made together. I can still
hear his strange and familiar songs. I remember Ben's
capacity for seeing the sun behind the clouds, his quick
temper and his gift of memory snap as he called it.

There is one other thing. You must understand that Ben
is not like you and me.

Ben is a mole.

Chapter Two

I discovered the place by accident. As you know, small boys
are often merciless and will take any chance to make
mischief. I was no exception. I was with a friend one summer's day, a day so dry I heard the corn cracking in the
heat. I had spent the morning on the high downs turning
over stones, sitting still to catch lizards, tunnelling in the
long grass for voles, searching for creatures to add to my

zoo. By midday we came close to an old dewpond and watched from a distance the shepherd filling the troughs for the
sheep. Perhaps it was the heat, or perhaps a slow-worm had
been too quick for me, but I was in the mood for mischief
and so was my friend. We waited for the shepherd to go
before coming from our hiding place. We took two stakes
from a fence, two heavy ones with sharp points. We were
going to spike the dewpond, a game like hedgin', for little
boys only.

I should tell you about dewponds as they were rare when I

was a boy. Piped water put an end to them, but in the wilder places you could still find one with grass growing over the edges and algae swimming on the surface. It was the age-old way of getting water to the sheep. Today the art is forgotten, though I have heard of a family at Lambourne who keep the secret but have no call to practise it. The favourite site was a depression on a high place. It was dug out so it sloped like a pyramid upside down, and it was as deep in the middle as a man standing. This was packed with dry wheatstraw, then puddled thickly with clay. The shepherd fenced it off and filled the troughs so the sheep did not break the clay lining.

We knew its weakness, too, so we were careful to choose long stakes. We threw them as high as possible and watched them land. The first fell too broadly to do any damage, but the second hit the right angle and almost disappeared. We watched as the chalk sucked the dewpond dry, then, forgetting our fears, yelped and cried in triumph around the pond. The shepherd must have heard our cries for he appeared above the distant ridge. He was running towards us.

We fled like sparrows from the wings of a hawk, down the straight track, across the plain, flat out for the vale slopes where we could vanish in any of the small valleys. We parted to give one of us a chance, and, as ill-luck had it, it was my trail the shepherd followed. I ran my feet out but the shepherd, used to the hard ways, closed the gap. I ran down the slopes of Ram's Hill, careless of the boulders and brambles which tore at my legs. I scrambled over a fence and into a ditch. But he had seen me. I nearly cartwheeled down the slope, my ears buzzing with the bees which flew up from the flowers. I tottered on a ridge and saw a grove of thorns below me. I saw the level ground beyond it, and farther still the trees of Combe Springs Wood. I could hear the shepherd close behind me. I darted to my left where a winter stream cut a way down the slope. I slid and scrambled down this, startling a white bird from the thorn grove. I needed a place to hide. I crawled into the trees and hid among the shadows. I listened to the shepherd's curses and the fate he had planned when he caught me. I heard his heavy breathing on the ridge top. I hid behind a large block of sarsen stone.

"Now I've got you," cried a voice. The shepherd scrambled down the slope.

I pressed against the stone and must have pushed so hard that I put my foot through the ground. I had sprained my ankle and I could feel it dangling in mid-air in some sort of tunnel. I wanted to get away. I pulled the turf from the stone but it was too late. The shepherd had crawled through the trees and grabbed my shirt. I was a country boy and put up a fight. I clutched the turf with both hands as he pulled me clear. The sides gave way and I was hauled out and given a sound thrashing.

*　　*　　*　　*　　*

It was not long with the cares and wiles of little boys that the episode was forgotten, even the thrashing, though the thought of it was always painful. I avoided the high downs, preferring to explore the meadows around our farm. I suppose I did once or twice think of the hole under the stone, but rather in the way I see a face in a crowd, clearly one moment, then lost in the others the next.

Two weeks later my mother called me from the bottom of the kitchen garden where I was feeding flies to my bull toad. I knew it was trouble by the sound of her voice. I knew I was innocent, more or less, though I had taken half a cake, in little slices, and sold my mother's thimble to a tinker the month before. But I was sure she had not noticed.

She held me by the shoulders and asked me to look at her.

"How many times baa lamb (a name she sometimes called me) have I told you not to put stones in your pocket?"

I looked at a pile of washing on the table.

Her blue eyes sparkled with suspicion as she pulled something from her apron pocket.

"And where did baa lamb find this? In a cowpie?" She paused. "If you don't tell the truth, the bogey he'll come and get you."

She opened her hand. There was a square stone in it, or something that looked like stone only it was whiter. I had never heard of ivory then. There were lots of scratches on both sides as if it had been carved by a sharp instrument. It

14

looked very old.

I told her I had never seen it before, and when she said she had found it in the wash, I was genuinely surprised. She was not surprised. I could not say how it had got there. My clothes were washed only when the basket was full, and, as I wore clothes till my mother pulled them off me, I had lost all sense of time.

My mother gave me back the stone as she did not want it, and told me not to do it again as it ruined the pockets. I kept the stone in my bedroom and used it to play heads and tails, for on one side there was a kind of circle, and on the other a tail if you looked at it the right way.

That summer during the holidays I was kept busy on the farm. I was as happy as a lark, proud to be doing a man's job alongside my elder brothers. The autumn came soon enough, the beeches turned and the meadows filled with mist on cold nights. It smelt good for mushrooms, but the white-out we expected every year in Primrose Meadow had hardly started when the frost came. That put an end to that. There was enough ice at Martinmas to skate on Kingston Lisle pond, and what a time we had of it! And when the snow came early, I jumped for joy. My grandfather nodded his head gravely. The road to Lambourn was blocked by early December, but we did not suffer as our parish was well served by other routes. Even our dogs had a better time of it than the strangers which passed through our village. It was about that time that I heard the story of Uncle Jacob and his donkey.

Uncle Jacob was a hermit who lived in a crumbling cottage on the high downs above Woolstone. He was a stubborn old man and refused every offer to take an almshouse in Uffington. He preferred his farmworker's cottage, with the flagstone floors and the byre at the back where he kept his only companion, a donkey. So close were they, and so seldom were they parted, that it was said they both smelt the same. Though Uncle Jacob liked his solitude—his nearest neighbour was over a mile away—he was forced to collect his supplies from Woolstone. When the snow cut off the hill road, the old man struggled through on his donkey. He collected his supplies and said goodbye to the storekeeper. He was never seen alive again. A search party found him halfway home, at the bottom of an eight-foot drift. His devoted donkey was still going round in circles, pausing every time he stepped over his master to lick the snow from his face.

By Christmas the parish was at a standstill. The snow was as high as the garden gate and it took all day for my father to feed the cattle. Then one night it thawed, and three of the cows fell in a ditch and drowned. The winter barley was swept away, but I was more upset when I went to the bottom of the garden. I had lost half my zoo in the flood.

In February the starlings arrived. Everyone saw the tight, dark flocks flying by day over the bleak fields, roosting by night at Blowingstone Wood. It was said that you could hear their nightly cackle from as far as Uffington. My father took me once to see them rise from the wood, a morning spectacle that had drawn comment in the local broadsheet. Their chatter rose with the sun as if the wind was chasing leaves through the trees. Then there was silence . . . then *whoof* . . . they were up, one huge bird darkening the sky, conjuring with shapes as a magician does, rising one moment, shelving the next, changing from a saucer to a mushroom, clouds to rainfall.

No-one minded the starlings, until other flocks appeared and their number multiplied in a matter of days. No-one knew where they came from, and when they started foraging in the barley fields, my father became worried. He said they were thriving to spite us, and it was then, I suppose, the mood changed and the cry of blood was heard.

My father was one of the party—there were twenty my

brother told me—that went to Blowingstone Wood armed with guns. They went there before sunrise while the birds were massed together. They went there every morning for a week. Lots of boys followed with their catapults. I remember the hundreds of crows and magpies which feasted there for a week after. No-one minded that though, except when the wind blew off the downs to remind us of the killing. Of course, that was the end of the starlings and we were glad to forget the past.

I rarely come across anyone who remembers the starlings. An isolated misfortune, I have been told. I thought so at the time, but to forget the past is to live in peril. We easily forget things we do not understand. After the starlings went (how nicely the memory puts these things) something of the cream-and-butter days returned. The ground drained quickly with the milder weather and my father was able to make good a lot of the sowing. The grass came on early, and there were no harsh frosts.

Everything was as it should be and my grandfather said so, too. The daffodils were on the verge of flowering and so were the tree buds; the barley shoots had appeared, the ewes were ready to lamb, when a short notice appeared in the broadsheet. It was from a local naturalist saying that he had not yet heard a cuckoo or seen a swallow. It passed without comment in our family, for it was one of those things no-one really thought about. Two weeks passed and the daffodils had still not bloomed and nor had the trees; the ewes were still about to lamb and the barley had not grown any more. A second letter appeared in the broadsheet from the naturalist. He reported that nowhere in the Uffington district had a swallow been seen or a cuckoo heard.

Most people that I heard talking on the subject had their own explanation. 'Ah well, there's nature for you!' Another would add: 'Always got a trick up her sleeve.' The subject was soon forgotten, except, of course, by the naturalist who made himself unpopular by suggesting that too many of the woods had been cleared and the swallows had nowhere to hibernate. (This was in the days when some still thought that swallows hibernated!)

It rained so hard at Easter that the Morris men cancelled

the dancing and my father joined them in the local pub. The village was full of worried faces a week later. The daffodils had still not flowered, the buds on the trees had not opened, the ewes had not lambed and the barley shoots were still tiny in the fields. For the first time my father bought in hay for the cattle as the grass had stopped growing. It was all put down to the cold weather, but more than that no-one would say. A silence surrounded the subject as thick as any mist.

I remember the day well. It was a Sunday and I had my father's permission to spend the afternoon collecting animals for my zoo. I walked without a plan or so I thought. I took the track through Combe Springs Wood, hardly pausing until I reached the lonely valleys below Ram's Hill. I wandered up and down the slopes, keeping to the sheep and hare tracks where possible, and finally sat on a ridge. I looked down on the thorngrove where the shepherd had once trapped me.

I noticed that the thorns were bare, unlike the last time when they were a dark cloak peppered with red berries. I could see clearly the big sarsen stone in the middle. I was startled by a white bird, heavily built like a rook, which flew out from the far side of the grove. I watched it flap lazily above the distant slopes, before it circled in a wide arc to disappear towards Britchcombe Wood. I held my breath when I saw something move in the shadows by the stone. It was small, dark and pointed. It clambered across the top of the stone, then it stood on a short pair of legs. It was a mole and it was dancing.

It held me as a finger holds a ring. I could not take my eyes off this swaying creature. I could see its black fur rippling as it strained and stretched with its claws, bending so far back I thought it would topple; but each time it righted itself, sweeping its smaller foreclaws over the stone so the grove rung with faint rattling sounds. The mole squatted on the stone, drawing its pointed head into its chest. It seemed to be sniffing, for its snout and whiskers went from side to side in quick, nervous movements. It stood again and turned in my direction. I hardly dared to breathe. A gun fired at that moment in a distant valley. I heard a dog barking. The mole vanished down the side of the stone.

When I got home later that day I swore I would not be happy until I had the mole in my hands, and that meant in my zoo. One thing leads to another, and as sure as the little wolf spider hunts its prey with patience, cunning and endurance, I planned to catch my prey. Though I was a minnow, I had the hunter's heart which wanted to possess, to hold the thing so far from my reach, to feel its warmth and heart beating. I wanted it to be mine. I thought of it night and day. I kept it a secret to myself.

I was so busy planning how to catch the dancing mole that I hardly noticed the mist which appeared after Easter. At first it covered the meadows in the early morning to vanish by midday. Then it spread to the winter barley and after a week it had reached the kitchen garden to slowly disappear during the day until the evening, when the tide turned, and it came back again. Unlike the rest of the family, I saw the mist as a friend for I used it as cover to crawl close to the stone.

I thought of every scheme to catch the mole. I sprinkled worms on the stone. I made a special trap to fly over and cover the mole at the slightest touch, but I gave that up when my father boxed my ears for ruining the cabbage net. I even learnt to count as far as seventy eight, for that was as long as I could sit in silence. I spent all my spare time at Thorngrove waiting and watching—but without any success. It was then, when I knew that the mole had outwitted me, I decided to look for him in his lair. I waited for a Sunday, a day I had no chores, and set out to explore the tunnel.

I did not waste time when I reached the stone. I used a hand-fork to widen the hole I had made the summer before. I was surprised at how easily the soil came away. I dug the hole big enough to peer through with my head. It was larger than I thought. I shone a lamp into the hole but all I could see were twisted roots and dark shadows. I never imagined it could be so big. I made sure that my belt pouch was closed and tucked in my jumper. I finished a chocolate biscuit and then slid in slowly head first.

The air was musty and damp. I shone the lamp around me, while still lying on my belly. There was a tangle of roots above but the tunnel sides were smooth. The taproots had been cut neatly away. There was a faint breeze on my face. I shone the lamp in its direction. There was a tunnel, a large tunnel, ahead of me. I held the torch in one hand and kicked gently to push myself towards it. I was surprised how easy it was to move. I kicked a little harder. Some earth fell on top of me. I started to cough. I kicked away at the roots . . . stones fell on my shoulder. I heard a rushing in my ears. I kicked violently to get clear.

The stone caved in . . .

Chapter Three

I was surprisingly calm. I had lost my lamp and could not see because of the darkness. I had difficulty breathing because of the dust. Behind me I sensed the weight and confusion of the collapsed tunnel. I stretched my fingers, my shoulders and my legs. I turned my head and curled my toes. I was in one piece. I lay face down wondering what to do. I felt for my torch but could not find it. I knew it was hopeless to try and dig my way out. But somehow it did not matter. I felt very detached from it all. I pulled myself forward, testing every grip to make sure it was firm. I could see a faint light ahead of me. It was not sunlight, I was sure. It was coming from the tunnel sides where they met the roof. The light came from different points, and they were spaced evenly apart. I could see them clearly now. They came from small rocks wedged into the sides. I felt one and it was hard and polished like a piece of crystal.

I was astonished to find how smooth the sides were, as if they had been rubbed that way by constant use. I was full of misgivings and excited butterflies. I wanted to escape and I wanted to explore. I listened to the drumming of my heart and my rapid breathing. If I moved my hand, the sound echoed around my head. I had no fear of suffocating for a draught tickled my nose with its coolness. I thought that if I followed the breeze I would find my way out. And that is what I did.

The tunnel kept a winding course as if tracing the contours of a valley. I contorted myself like a weasel once to pass under a shelving roof, otherwise I crawled comfortably without fear of banging my head. Do not think me particularly brave if I have skimmed over my feelings. A passion had taken me into the tunnel and I was still in its grip. I had no time to worry, for being trapped underground is no place for imagining things.

I knew long before I arrived that the tunnel had ended. The draught was stronger and cooler, and the echoes were louder, bouncing back steadily at shorter intervals from something solid. Instead of the wall of earth I had expected, the tunnel ended against a tree trunk. I did not have to tap the sides to know this. I could see with my own eyes. There were so many polished stone lights it looked like a starry night sky.

I lay there wondering what to do, when a shrill, angry sound caught my attention. It came from the tunnel side in front of me. I heard it again:

"Kuuuuuuuuuuuuuushi wuuuuuuuuuuuushi cooooooooo-rooooooooo". Silence, and then again. "*Ooooooooooooooooo-oooooooooshi wuuuuuushi coooo.*"

I pinpointed the source. I thought it was a large tree root, but when I looked closer, I saw it was too square, too un-natural. I shuddered as I felt a door. There were hinges on one side. There was also a handle.

The high whistling voice continued, no longer loudly, but fainter and fainter as if it was on the move.

"Miiiiiiiiiilkeeeeee time Slither. Miiiiiiiiilkeeeeee."

I kept absolutely quiet. I ran my hands along the door again. It was a ragged square door, unexpectedly large, about the size of two quart bottles put together. The edges were uneven as if they had been chewed in a hurry or a temper. I hardly heard the voice now. I wondered who it could be. My courage returned. I ran my hand over the door and to my astonishment discovered some carvings. I felt a square and a circle at the top of the door which I did not understand, along with several other strange markings. It was hard to read by that light, but even a blind man can feel letters. The words were carved in the same ragged edges as the door. They said:

BEN THE MOLE
PRIVATE DETECTIVE
BY APPOINTMENT ONLY

There was another sign below this warning:

BEWARE OF THE SLUG

I cannot describe my feelings then. It was all familiar in a strange way. As if I had been feeling in the dark for something I could not see, but finding it because I knew it was there.

I pressed my ear against the door. I heard the voice from a great distance. I took a big breath and pushed open the door.

*   *   *   *   *

I was in a large chamber lit brightly in four corners by piles of the same polished stones. I could not see the roof or into the shadows beyond the lights. The place was alive with shadows and flickering light-beams. They flashed between the corner-stone lights, pulsing on and off so they appeared to be moving like the cartoons of the magic lanterns. The centre of the room was much darker, occasionally lit by a bright light when I would see the straw scattered on the floor and a table.

I crouched in the shadows listening and watching, suspecting every sound to be the approach of the householder. I did not have to wait long. I held my breath as a huge shadow, pointed at the top, barrel-shaped at the bottom, appeared on the far wall. It travelled slowly nearer, a looming figure pulsing from side to side but never losing its shape. In an outstretched claw it held a large bowl. I sank into the straw as the footfalls and shuffles filled my senses. I was not prepared for giant moles. Its squeaking voice sounded like trumpet notes to my ears. It was angry and snorting.

"Slither. Where are you?"

I might have passed out with fear had I not noticed something else. It was a small, pointed shape travelling some distance back from the shadow. It was holding a saucer and swinging it from side to side. My giant mole was nothing more than its shadow. I still trembled, but this time with excitement as I recognised the dancing mole of the stone. I was puzzled how I could have mistaken it for a giant when it was only a few yards away. If I was puzzled, I was also scheming how to trap him in his lair.

The mole had stopped halfway along the opposite wall. It yawned through its front claws and peered among the shadows and light-beams. It looked up and down in short, fast movements. It snorted and put the saucer down. It seemed to be licking the bowl.

"*Mmmmmmmmmmmmmmmmmm* lovely," it squeaked through clenched teeth.

The mole fanned his whiskers to catch the slightest sound. His voice got shriller as its temper worsened.

"Master Ben is a detective and he knows you're there." He tried to be reasonable. "If you won't come down, he will have to come and get you."

The mole dropped on all fours. He was trembling with

anger. His stumpy tail beat against the straw. He pretended once more to lick his bowl.

"*Toad's bellies,*" he snorted suddenly, rapping his claws at the shadows. "*Come down, do you hear.*"

There was no sign of any movement.

"*Alright, alright.* I've had enough." He shuffled with great sweeps of his claws across the straw to the far pile of rock lights. He disappeared through another door. I heard angry mutterings echoing in the tunnel. The door was flung open and he reappeared with what looked like a rusty skewer in his right claw. He was incensed. His breath misted as he spoke.

"I'm going to count to ten and ten only. One . . . two . . . three (he held the skewer menacingly against the wall) . . . four . . . five . . . six. I'm serious . . ." He never finished. He lashed out with the skewer and knocked a big white slug from a ledge. He gobbled it down in two mouthfuls.

I was speechless. I was outraged. A frog of feelings caught in my throat. Instead of grabbing the mole, I jumped from the straw and shouted "That's terrible, just terrible. It was only a poor slug. How could you do it?"

The mole dropped to the floor and with three sharp breast-strokes buried himself in the straw so only his snout stuck out. It was twitching at me.

I crawled nearer, getting ready to pounce. I was about to spring when he did something which stopped me in my tracks. He got up calmly from the straw, brushing pieces from his shoulders and his chest. He looked into my eyes, and said abruptly, but not unkindly, "You're late."

Late? I did not know what to say. I sat down dumb-founded.

He fanned his whiskers and rotated his head in a small arc as if he was looking closely at me. He peered over his shoulders and then back to me.

"I hope it's not too small for you here." No sooner had he spoken than the corner lights got brighter, chasing the shadows farther away. The room got bigger.

"Is it big enough now?"

I nodded stupidly.

"You must excuse me," continued the mole in a high,

squeaking voice, "if I did not welcome you properly but I was busy . . . a tiresome business. Besides, you startled me."

I nodded, still unable to speak.

"As you can see, I have been having some trouble with my servant Slither."

"But you ate him," I burst out, recovering some of my outrage.

"Of course I did. Wouldn't you have done the same? He's been nothing but trouble ever since I took him on. He sleeps on the job. He steals food when I am not looking. What's more, he talks in his sleep."

"There must be something good about him," I said, feeling less outraged.

He scratched his whiskers with his claw. "I will say he did his job well nibbling all the things that grow on the walls. But he was a slimy character and I will not stand for disobedience."

"But you ate him," I persisted.

"Oh don't worry about that," he said pleasantly. "There are plenty more slugs."

I thought I would take him then, but he forestalled me with his quickfire thoughts.

"Did you bring any luggage?"

I shook my head.

"Good," he said rubbing his foreclaws together so they rattled with approval." How thoughtful, and so many do, you know. They just don't stop to think."

He peered at me confidingly, almost paternally. "And they can't take it with them."

I was revolted by his patronising manner, talking to me as if I was a child. Well, I was a child, but I was not going to be talked down to by a mole.

"What makes you think I'm staying in this hole anyway. I'm lost, that's all. Besides," I said more defiantly, "I have come to get you for my zoo."

The mole scratched his forehead, pushing the fur one way and then the other, an oddity with these creatures.

"I don't think you quite understand," he said at last. "Will you relax?"

I obeyed him like a puppet and sat on the straw opposite him across the table. I had the uncanny feeling that, though I knew I was much bigger than the mole, we were looking into each other's eyes.

"Forgive me for asking," said the mole, "but do you know where we are?"

I thought it was a trick question, so I played safe. "Underground, of course."

"I see," said the mole, fiddling with his whiskers the way our family doctor tugged his moustache.

"Will you feel your pulse then."

"Are you trying to frighten me," I said, for I had spirit in me. I obeyed him all the same.

"It's beating rather fast," I said anxiously.

"Exactly. Anything else?" he watched me carefully as I strained my senses. I heard a lot of buzzing but it was all too far or too near to put into words.

"Is it silence?" I said. I felt my body tingling, and the way I breathed less, the more I listened; and the more I listened, the more I could hear my heart. It was beating slower. I listened to it for a long while. I began to feel lighter. I wanted to fall asleep. I thought I heard a summer's day on the Downs when millions of insects hover in the sunlight. It grew stronger with the listening.

"It's a humming sound . . . and it's in my ears."

"Exactly," said Ben. "It's all around us . . . everywhere."

I jumped up from the straw. "Are you out of your mind?" I burst out.

"No," sighed the mole, "but I'm afraid you are not quite there yet but . . ." He startled me by jumping up. "There is much to do, tunnels to clean, worms to catch, lessons . . ."

"Lessons," I shouted, staring into his quizzical face. I tried to be reasonable. "Look, I don't know what's happening here, but I am a human being and you're a mole. Right?"

The mole said nothing.

I ran out of thoughts. "I think it's time I left." The corner lights dimmed as I spoke. I turned to leave by the door I had entered. The mole had a smilecrease across his whiskers.

It was here, I must warn you, that things became unhinged. If the room was strange, it grew stranger still. As I said, I turned to leave, and I turned again, and again and again. Everything looked the same. I said nothing as I did not wish to reveal my doubts. I chose one of the rocklights at random and crawled towards it. The pile of stones got brighter. The shadows receded. I crawled on all fours keeping my head down in case I banged it against the ceiling. I crawled until I thought I would drop but I was still no more than halfway to the lights. I turned round and in three strides I was back at the table. I said nothing to the mole but set off in the opposite direction. This time I watched the rocklights and crawled steadily towards them. These, too, got brighter and with every move the shadows were chased farther from me. I turned round and in three strides I was back at the table.

I kept a hold on myself and decided that the best thing was to pretend that I had changed my mind.

"I have been thinking," I told the mole as I sat opposite him. "This looks quite a cosy place. The shadows are really interesting. I've just been admiring them. I wouldn't mind staying here, perhaps help out a little bit now that Slither's gone." I gulped as I remembered Slither.

"Yes," I continued, "I don't eat much or talk in my sleep. I would like to stay for a while."

"Wonderful," squeaked the mole, squeezing his claws together. "I'd hoped you would change your mind. It's very hard to get good servants these days. Most of them are thoroughly unreliable. And you can't tell, even if they're from good families. I once had a stag beetle. He was a marvellous servant, except he lied all the time." He wrung his claws as he remembered the beetle.

"What happened to him?" I asked.

"Mmmmmmm," sighed the mole savouring the memory. "Was it breakfast or tea . . . or supper?" He peered at me, and through his sharp little teeth, asked, "You don't lie, do you?"

"Of course not," I lied.

"Good," said the mole. He jumped from the straw and

stretched a claw across the table. "But I haven't introduced myself. My name is Ben the mole. I am a private detective. And yours?"

"Fellman Clack, sir . . . at your service."

Chapter Four

I was informed politely yet firmly that now was not the time for more questions. There was work to be done. Ben said he had to inspect the tunnels, repair a trap and catch dinner. When I offered to help, thinking that is what a servant should do, I was told to explore the chamber.

"One more thing," he said before entering the doorway where he had found the skewer, "whatever you do, think big." The door slammed and I was alone.

You must imagine my thoughts. I sat in a daze unable to think the simplest things. What was happening to me? I went through every detail of the day. The mole was real enough. I picked his skewer from the table, but that filled me with misgiving. I knew I was bigger than a mole but the skewer was heavy in my hand. I pinched myself. That was real enough. I searched my pouch and pockets, and pulled out my box of matches and a chocolate biscuit. That tasted real enough. I banged the table and my hand hurt. I looked round the chamber and at each of the corner lights. The shadows fluttered around the walls, sometimes flashing in the darkness around me. I imagined the chamber was not a room at all, but a cave hollowed by underground streams. I listened and thought I heard a faint, rushing sound. I decided to explore.

I reached the distant rocklights in three or four strides. They were piled as high as my waist. The rocks, crystals or whatever they were, had been flung carelessly on top of each other; they were all shapes, from bits the size of sixpences to some as big as apples. They flickered at different rates, and it was this that created the shadows and lightbeams which danced around the chamber. I had thought that the light was white, but now that I watched carefully I could see the occasional traces of green. "Fancy that," I thought to myself, "green light." I had always played that game of guessing shapes in clouds, so it pleased me to imagine it was the colour of grass. Some of the shadows had darker edges and I thought these were the hedgerows between the fields. It was amazing what you could see into something. I saw clouds rolling over the fields, and I had to look twice when I saw a bird. It really looked like a bird. I knew it was just a shadow but it still startled me. I decided that I had had enough of looking at shadows and continued exploring the cavern.

I imagined it must have taken thousands of years to hollow a space this size. I could not see the ceiling and even when I stood on tiptoe it was beyond my reach. I walked back towards the table listening hard for the sound of running water. I detected a movement in the air around me as if something was hurrying in a confined space. The door burst open and a dark, pointed shape swam a clumsy breast-stroke over the straw straight to the table.

I was disgusted by what I saw next. The mole pulled about twenty wriggling worms from a skewer on which they were tied. He piled them on the table in front of him. He counted them one by one until he reached twenty. It was grotesque. He held the side of the table with his foreclaws, and then he sucked them one by one until they were all gone. He sat back on the straw and played with his whiskers.

"Nothing like dinner," he squeaked contentedly.

I was revolted by this display. I would have left the table had I not been his servant. Instead, I indulged in the courage of feeling superior.

"Haven't you got any manners?"

He scratched his fur one way and then the other. "Manners," he said pausing to consider the word. "Can you eat them?"

"Of course you can't. They're what you do when people are around."

"Ah," said Ben thoughtfully. "Who's people?"

"I'm a people and you are a mole."

He looked even more puzzled. I got more angry. I picked

31

up my foot and held it above the table. "That's a foot, see."
I waved my hand. "That's a hand." I pointed to myself.
"Person. I'm a person." I pointed to him. "Creature.
You're a creature and creatures eat worms. Persons," I said
banging my chest, "eat sausages."

Ben was not upset at all, on the contrary, he was very interested in sausages. He had never heard of sausages and
asked me to describe them. He got up suddenly and hurtled
across the straw to the rock lights. A tunnel door slammed.
It opened almost immediately and there was a flurry in the
straw and a dark, pointed shape popped up by the table. On
his worm stick was a string of sausages. They looked just
like my mother's home-made chipolatas. I knew it was a
trick so pretended to ignore him. Ben took the sausages
from the stick and spread them before me. I could smell a
familiar mixture of sweet and savoury herbs.

"Sausages," said Ben smilecreasing his whiskers.

I knew he was trying to frighten me so I kept a straight
face. I looked at the sausages. They looked like sausages. I
touched one. It felt like a sausage. I smelt it. It smelt like a
sausage. I tasted one and spat it out.

"It's not cooked."

"Cooked?" said Ben puzzled. "What is cooked?"

I talked to him in pidgin English, raising my voice to help
him understand. "*Fire,*" I said rubbing my hands, "it
needs fire."

He looked blankly at me. "What is fire?"

I knew he was too stupid to understand, so I took my
matches from my pouch. Ben was interested in my pouch
and how it was made. I struck the match on the table. Ben
quivered as though he had had an electric shock. He sat
rigidly, then fell back with his claws sticking in the air. He
had passed out. I crawled round the table and gently slapped
his face. His whiskers, which had gone slack, stiffened and
he sprung up like a jack-in-the-box.

"Where was I?" he said. His claws touched the sausages
on the table. "Ah. Cooked sausages, your favourite dish I
understand."

I was horrified and delighted. They were cooked. After
that I never asked questions about food but learnt to enjoy

what was put before me.

*   *   *   *   *

I discovered that a mole is a creature of habit. Though it had never heard of time or watches, it had a precise pattern, as regular as the sunrise and sunset which we never saw. He slept three times a day in a special pile of straw under the table. He always had breakfast in bed from a supply of dried worms by his bedside. After this he went back to sleep until he woke the second time. Then he had another snack of dried worms which he first counted, banging once on the table for each worm. I knew when he was getting up, for after twenty knocks the straw flew away from under the table along with Ben. He always said, ''What a lovely night!''

He was as vain as a peacock and had a morning ritual of sitting on the table and sharpening his claws on a stone until they were fine points. Then he would inspect them, one by one, rubbing them against each other to feel the sharpness. He washed himself by spitting on his claws and then running them through his dark velvety fur, pushing the fur one way and then another, handy for travelling backwards or in a tight corner.

At first I was glad to have nothing to do. It reminded me of holidays. I spent my time exploring the cavern, and if I was not doing this, I wondered where Ben went and what his business could be. He said he was a detective but we never had any visitors, or none that I saw. In the end I was forced to the conclusion that Ben and I were the sole inhabitants of the cave. It would have been a spidery thought had I not grown, how can I say it, to enjoy his company. There was always an opportunity to talk over dinner when he had returned from the tunnel and before his third sleep. I had thought him stupid but I was changing my mind. He was just uneducated, with a very limited vocabulary. He could only count to twenty.

I was immensely curious about him, what made him tick, how he had found the cavern and many other questions that filled a boy's mind. I discovered that he had no sense of time, only a great sense of habit. He forgot something as soon as he said or did it, as when he fainted from the lighted match. But the far past, the ancestral memories, flowed easily into his small talk as if they had happened yesterday. I thought he lived in the past and told him so. He should look to the future. "Future," he said, "is like worm pie, but first you have to catch the worms."

Often, in our conversations, he mentioned his great-great-great-great-great-grandmole Wormhole the First. He had originally lived in the barley strips of the Vale, somewhere close to Combe Springs Wood. I think Ben thought he was like Wormhole, for he took every opportunity to describe in greater and greater detail how Wormhole had started the tunnels at Thorngrove. Once the family estate, which Ben inherited as the eldest male, was so vast that his grandmole Wernte could travel and sleep for three days and still not see all the property. Now only a small part was maintained, the rest having fallen into disuse, blocked by roots and cobwebs, or taken over by streams or flitter mice. Ben still 'farmed', if that is the right word, though he liked to keep it to a minimum because of his business. Besides, he told me once, it was getting harder and harder to find good worm-catchers and tunnel-repairers. He preferred to live alone and conduct his business on the same lines established by Wormhole. Whenever I questioned him about this, he feigned sleepiness and retired to bed.

34

I should say another thing, striking really, but one I never noticed as it was so obvious. When I entered his office, I had the soft, freckled skin of a boy, but in no time it was dark, not dirty exactly, but worn and hard like my father's hands. I did my best to stay clean but as the only running water was far away in the cavern, I relied on spitting into my hands and rubbing it into my skin.

I did this automatically until I discovered with a shock that I was copying Ben, combing my hair with my fingers, sharpening my nails on stones and scratching my body for fleas. I slept three times a day, had breakfast in bed, usually sausages; in short, I ordered my life as my master did. This did not disturb me too much as I knew I was people and Ben was a mole. What disturbed me was that I kept forgetting it.

* * * * *

My education began in earnest over one dinner. I said casually: "When I came here you mentioned lessons. Well, I haven't had any."

Ben broke off from guzzling a worm. He wiped his whiskers. He had a pained look on his face, then fur folds of temper. "Lessons," he squeaked, rapping his claws on the table, "you've already started your lessons."

There was a long silence as we stared at each other across the table. Ben leaned on his claw and asked his erring servant in a gentler, resigned voice: "Where do I go when I leave you?"

"On business," I said remembering his own words.

"And where's that?"

"Down the tunnel."

"I see," he sighed. He paused. "What if I told you my business is your business?"

"Impossible," I replied indignantly, "you're never here."

"Ah," said Ben, jumping up from the straw and leaning closer to me. "So that's what the little one thinks, is it?"

"Yes, it is," I said bravely. His patronising manner brought out the fighter in me.

"*Right.*" He pressed his claws against his sides. He shuffled back several paces, keeping his eyes on me. He stopped and sat down on the straw. "Now clever one, watch me."

I watched him, sure that I would make him eat his words. He sat in a pyramid shape, his pointed head and snout balancing on his round body. I watched as the light flickered on his dark velvety fur. His shadow wavered on the straw in time to the passing lights. I kept him in sight but I had to strain to keep my eyes focused. I never realised that the straw was so deep. Ben seemed to be sinking into it. I wondered what trick he was planning. I kept my eyes steadily on him. I had to blink to believe the thought. It was true, he was sinking into the straw. It was up to his middle. I was so sharply focused that I had not seen it was the straw which was rising. It reached his chest, covering his shoulders and neck. His whiskers became strands of straw. It covered his head.

Ben disappeared. There was nothing left but a pile of straw.

"All right. Very clever," I said. "You can come out now." There was no answer. I was not going to be tricked so easily. I crawled round the table and punched the heap of straw. It flew into a hundred pieces. I panicked. I picked large handfuls of straw. There was nothing there. I sat down astonished.

"Ouch!"

I jumped up again. The straw was moving. I could see whiskers. It was Ben. He was groaning and rubbing the side of his face.

I was not apologetic. We sat opposite each other at the table. Ben was still rubbing the side of his face.

"That, little one, is the first lesson in the art of disappearing, a lesson you will have to master if you are to be of any help. It is the lesson of sitting stone, and, without it," he added ominously, "you will be a sitting duck for any hoverhawk." He paused for his words to take effect.

"Any questions?"

I was flabbergasted. I did not know if I had been deceived or had witnessed a master detective at work. My mind teemed with questions like flies on a donkey's back. If I had had a stumpy tail, I would have banged it with frustration; instead I banged the table with my fist.

"I don't know what to think."

He curled his whiskers in a slightly superior manner. "Good. You have been so busy looking at me that you did not see where I went. This is right?"

I nodded.

"Likewise there are so many thoughts you don't know what to think."

I nodded again.

"That is a subject we shall return to. Lesson over."

* * * * *

I mention this curious episode, for that is how it appeared to me, to show the provocative, authoritative way Ben put things. He made me think, and for a boy that is no small thing. As I have said, I thought him intelligent but uneducated. A beast with redeeming features. I don't know what I thought of him then, but I knew our relationship was changing. I was a servant and something else. I found out the following day.

There was enough light to see each other but not into the gloom as we sat around the table after dinner. Ben finished rattling his claws against each other and asked abruptly:

"Any questions?"

For once I was prepared. I had always been puzzled by his detective sign outside his office entrance. Yet I had never seen any callers. I asked him why.

"You are mistaken," he said with conviction. "Why, I am busy on a case now."

"Whose case?"

"Yours."

"*Me?* I came here by mistake . . . well, I didn't quite plan it like this."

"Mistake? No such thing. I never make mistakes," said Ben. "Though you were a little late, that's true."

"Do you mean I am your client?"

"Exactly."

"I thought you said I was your servant."

"Exactly."

"I have come here to learn something?"

"Exactly."

This was getting boring. I got to the point.

"What have I come to learn?"

"Lessons, of course."

We were back where we started. It never dawned on me that I was his apprentice until he said it.

"You see Fellman, if you are to be of help, you must understand my ways. I deal with all sorts in this business and there are many who love nothing more than a little mole pie. I never give them the chance. Why? I'll tell you. Because I'm ready for the dangers. If I could count more than twenty, there would be an unaccountable number of times sitting stone has saved my life. The same is true of not-think, but more of that later. Ever since Flit the Wren left, I have needed a good apprentice to take over from me. But where do you find them? Everyone is busy, rush, rush, rush. The world is a vole's nest. No time for anything except rushing. Of course, it needs a lot of preparation. Many skills have to be mastered."

He sighed at some passing recollection.

"Yes, the business has always been in our family, handed down from Wormhole the First through the eldest moles of each generation. The tradition is unbroken, that is, until now. I have no offspring."

He changed the subject. "You say it was a mistake you came here. It's not true. When you saw me dancing on the ageless stone, did you think I had not seen you?"

My heart jumped. I was changing my picture of Ben every moment.

"There are ways in the hedgerows you do not yet understand. I knew a lot about you before you even saw me or knew I existed. I knew about your zoo. Do you remember the bull toad? The one you found in the sand bucket."

I nodded.

"Do you think it was in a bucket by chance? Believe me, it was no easy business. That poor toad had to practically follow you around for two days before you saw it. It was quite exhausted, so exhausted it sent no messages for a whole full moon. I have other friends, too. The white rook, for example. He had been watching you for several days. He is an excellent judge of character and I liked what he told me about you. Do you still think this is all a ghastly mistake?''

I could hear the blood rushing in my head. I said nothing.

''Yes, I liked what they told me about you. I thought to myself, here is my new apprentice. Then, it was a relatively simple matter to arrange for a visit.''

I chose my words carefully. ''Do you mean you led me here?''

''Exactly. I have my ways, as you see, and now you are here. I let you believe that you were a servant, otherwise it might have overwhelmed you. I didn't want that.''

I looked into his dim, rounded eyes, so small you had to know they were there to see them. I could not believe it had all been planned. That it was not I hunting the mole but the mole luring me. Then the creature opposite me was no ordinary mole but what he said he was, a master detective. My mind revolted against the idea but I knew in my heart that it was true . . . I wanted to laugh or cry. I felt so many things I was going to burst. I did the only thing a boy can do. I cried and cried so the tears ran down my face. Not tears of grief but tears of relief. I had found a meaning in this nightmare, a warm intelligence for my guide.

''Are you in pain?'' asked Ben.

''I'm crying because I'm happy,'' I gulped.

He sightwhiskered me, twitching his snout. ''Your face is wet. Have you cut yourself?''

''No, no,'' I shouted. ''I'm just happy. Don't you know what tears are?''

''Is it this?'' said Ben. He rolled on the straw clutching his sides and started squeaking as if a stoat was on his tail.

''Enough, enough,'' I laughed. I looked at my furry master. ''Don't you know what it is to be sad?''

He shook his whiskers.

''To feel empty and without hope. To feel lost and small. Then a little bit of light comes in and it's all gone. Just like that. And I feel happy and I want to cry.''

Ben continued shaking his whiskers. ''Strange. I've never heard of this crying. Is it catching?''

We were not getting very far. I tried another approach.

''What do you do when your best friend is gobbled up by a hoverhawk? What do you feel?''

Ben scratched his fur both ways. He stared blankly at the flickering shadows on the wall. I waited for an answer. I looked closer and saw that his whiskers were still, a sure sign that something was troubling him. His fur trembled. His claws rattled. His tail swished the straw in rapid, tiny beats. I felt smug for he looked on the brink of crying. He was sightwhiskering the wall corner by the rock lights. A shadow was hovering, almost as if it had wings. Remarkable, I thought to myself. It looked so real, just like a big hawk. As soon as I thought it, it moved slowly across the wall, slower than the other shadows, as if looking for something. I saw yellow flashes which could have been eyes. I saw darker edges which could have been claws. The black-and-white shadows fanned along the bottom of the wall, flowing in and out of each other just like stripes. "Fancy that," I thought, "it could almost be a badger." I was astonished by the likeness.

I tapped Ben on the shoulder. "Are you all right? Cat got your tongue?"

Ben toppled over. He lay flat on the straw.

I thought quickly and fished out some dried worms from his store under the table. I held one over his snout. He sucked it down and jerked upright.

"Where was I?" he squeaked cheerfully.

"With the hoverhawk," I said.

"Hoverhawk? Oooooo hoverhawk. Horrible." He brushed the straw from himself and stared at the wall. "I do hope Pickles is all right . . . "

"But it was only pretend."

He looked gravely at me. "Don't ever say things like that. Fortunately, I managed to not-think the hoverhawk, but it was a close thing." He kept muttering to himself, still sightwhiskering the wall.

I don't know if it was my imagination, but I swear I heard loud chomping sounds, as if something was being guzzled in a hurry. It came from the middle of the wall where the black-and-white shadows hovered as brightly as fireflies, dancing in and out of each other. I smiled at the tricks it played with my senses. For a moment I thought I saw a badger's face, and where a silver-streaked shadow curled, its broad pied back tucked against a darker wall. There were pinpricks of light shining through the shadows at the top of the wall. It looked just like a starry night sky. I heard slurping and gurgling sounds. I heard guzzling sounds, and a heavy scraping as if a paw was scooping up something. I heard Ben.

"The greedy thing. Always stuffing himself."

Chapter Five

Ben had a special voice for lessons. It amused me as I remembered the earnest schoolteacher and his serious monotone which went neither up nor down but quite straight as a flying rook. He spoke as if he was recalling something he had learnt by heart and was passing it on out of duty. I found his voice and manner patronising, especially the way he shuffled around the table with his elbows stuck out and claws thrust to his side.

The subject of the lesson, he informed me, was the art of seeing. I found this rather funny when I looked into his tiny eyes that only saw the shadows of things. He began grandly.

"In the art of detection as taught by Wormhole the First, a mole has to learn to see and not see—do you see what I mean?"

"Not really," I said.

He paused. "But first, one has to want to see. I remember a sad case. A moth came to see me, one of those with long tongues which love the sweet-smelling night flowers of honeysuckle and jasmine. This was a worried moth for I was told it couldn't see in the dark. And if you are a moth, that is a problem.

"I made sure its feelers were normal. They were. I asked the moth to fly around my office. Well, the little thing flew straight to the rock lights and stayed there. I called it back but it wouldn't come. It refused to move.

"Eventually, after many sweet words, it returned to the table. I noticed its feelers were shaking. It kept looking anxiously towards the light. I did a little more not-think and realised its problem in a flash. It was afraid of the dark, and a moth that is afraid of the dark is only half a moth."

I agreed.

"His problem was that he didn't want to see in the dark because he was frightened of it.

"So the art of seeing," he continued, "is much more than opening your eyes. You must first want to see."

"What happened to the moth?"

"Moth. What moth? Ah! I know moths are very stubborn and hate to change. I advised him to feed at dusk when there is a little sun and a little moon. It was all I could do."

Ben pointed to his eyes. "Seeing is much much more than that. I can only see you if I strain, but with this (he bristled his whiskers) I have a feely picture of you. When I sightwhisker, I can see things which are unaccountably small, things which are so small you can't see them." He paused to think of an example.

"What track starts deeply so the soil is kicked up around the edges, but as you follow the prints they become fuzzier, shallower, the strides are shorter, with breaks on the hind claws?"

I knew enough from my zoo hunting to answer correctly. It was a frightened creature which was tired or injured.

"Excellent," said Ben. "There are all kinds of seeing and a detective must be a master in them all." He tapped his snout. "I smell and taste with this, nearly the same thing. Every smell tells a story. A hunting fox has a definite smell and so has a frightened creature which is being hunted. There are fearless weasel smells, shy rabbit smells, horrible poohy smells, smells which will curl your snout like a dry leaf. There are spider shadow smells, smells which wake you in your sleep, spring smells, sweet smells and truffles. A detective must study all these things."

The mention of truffles excited him so his whiskers quivered and his tail thumped the floor. He looked like a lemonade bottle about to fizz.

"Ah! Of course. I remember now. Wormhole made a special study of this and he called it, 'A study in plantigrade foot smells'."

"Pardon?"

"Plantigrade smells, claws, paws, that sort of thing. A

hive of secrets handed down from grandmole to grandmole, and, perhaps, one day to you.''

''Where do you keep this study?'' I asked.

Ben pointed to the side of his head. ''It even describes a way of preserving smells, for just because you can't see the little beggars, doesn't mean you can't catch them.''

I asked how he did it.

He visibly puffed and I felt like clouting him on the snout, a most painful place for moles. Instead, I listened spellbound.

''Elementary, really. In my pouch which I take on business, I have a smellbox full of pine syrup. I dissolve the scents in this solution and heat it in the sun, or place it in the company of fireflies, until only the sweet crystals are left. Then, at my leisure, I identify the smell by eating the crystals.''

He smilecreased condescendingly. ''Perhaps I tire you with my researches?''

*   *   *   *   *

The lessons were held after the second breakfast of each day, after he had washed and before he disappeared down the skewer tunnel. He always got me to practise the art of disappearing or sitting stone (as he sometimes called it) stressing that it was a cornerstone of his methods. I must admit I had many failures for there is something about it which is hard for humans to grasp. It was not that it was difficult. Ben once said I could learn it instantly or practise it for twenty full moons and still not be able to do it. It was because there was a lot of unremembering to do.

It is hard to say exactly what sitting stone is or how to do it. It is like struggling to learn a song, then discovering that you can sing it by heart without having to remember anything. I can still sit stone to this day and have used it all my life, especially if I am discovered in a barn by the farmer. All I do is change into a bale of straw. I quickly discovered that sitting stone did not make you invisible or anything silly like that, but makes you part of wherever you are. If you are sitting on chestnut leaves, then you are chestnut leaves; if leaning against lichen-coloured rock, then you are the colours of lichen-coloured rock. I know there are creatures like certain lizards which do it naturally, but Ben had taken natural things and turned them into a science of a sort. I am still not sure how it works, but I know that without it Ben and many other creatures would not have the strength to travel so widely, for sometimes they use sitting stone instead of sleep, in order to recharge themselves.

Even if I did not care for his manner of teaching, seeing is believing, especially when my furry master turned into straw, table legs, a pile of worms, all at a moment's notice.

"Don't look so surprised," he told me the second time he did it. "This is no magic such as the owls use. To sit stone you have to know where you are and you must not wobble. That means seeing, listening and last of all, but most importantly, not-thinking."

He banged his claw on the table. "What did you hear?"

"A claw banging on the table," I replied.

His whiskers grimaced. "Try again." He banged his claw on the table.

"A claw banging on the table," I replied with not so much conviction.

He sighed a condescending sigh. "I am asking you to listen."

I watched carefully.

His right claw banged the table, while the free claw slapped his side.

"A claw banging a table and a claw slapping your side."

"Good," he murmured, "but did you hear me whistle?" Later he said: "You see, to sit stone or disappear at will a detective must know what is happening around him; then, with a little not-think, a hole is made inside and that is filled with whatever is closest—colours, smells, shapes and so on. It is simple really, but who has the patience to do it instantly?''

I agreed and knew I would get no nearer to understanding this mystery until I had mastered not-think. As I said earlier, I was never allowed out of Ben's office. When the master was away, I was left to explore the rock lights if I wished, sleep or simply wait for his return. I was given no tasks to do, not even menial ones, no housework or anything. Not that there was any work for me to do. There were no dishes to clean or wash, beds to make or lights to turn on or off. I started inventing jobs, but discovered that no sooner had I started polishing the table or brushing the straw flat than the job was finished. I even spent longer cleaning myself, or trying to eat twice as much at meals or sleeping twice as long. But it was no use. I still had the same amount of time to myself. In the end, to distract myself, I was forced to practise the art of disappearing, listening and thinking of questions to ask Ben at our next lesson.

I would spend hours (or so it seemed to me) trying to catch all the sounds, including the inside ones, my breathing, heartbeat, the rushing murmurs of my blood, the seashell hush in my mind. I learnt to see in a different way, too. I first noticed this with the table. I had always thought of it as a crude table and that is what I saw. Until one day I saw it differently. Instead of seeing the table first and its flat, hard edges, I saw the space within its shape, something I had always looked through before. It was solid and just as important as the four table legs. I was startled by this extra quality. The table was no longer a flat thing, but something filled with space. I had seen it three-dimensionally. I did not use these words at the time but was just aware of an extra quality as if there was more to it than I thought. I practised looking in this way and found even common things, such as a pile of straw, interesting.

Then one day I sat stone without realising it. I had been watching the table, knowing where I was as Ben had taught me, and I must have been so absorbed I did not hear the tunnel door slam and Ben swimming across the floor. He called me and I called back. He called again and I asked him not to shout as he was right beside me. We discovered the truth together; he hadn't seen me as I was part of the table.

How this had happened I still do not know. I felt no different being part of a table, in fact I remember it felt very steady and solid, as if my feet were firmly on the ground. Ben said nothing but, the next day, when he woke after his second sleep, he said off-handedly, ''I think it is time for not-think.''

I was very excited as I knew that not-think was a family secret passed down a long line of secretive detectives. I did not know what to expect, as Ben avoided the subject, occasionally hinting that only fools or master detectives could master it.

I waited with excited butterflies in my tummy. Ben shuffled around the table like the schoolteacher with his elbows out and claws thrust to his sides. I say shuffled but it was more like strutted. I became suspicious when he asked casually, addressing the darkness above our heads rather than me, to think of anything I wanted but not tell him.

''Now,'' he said, ''I will tell you what it is.''

I had got him at last, I thought. ''Impossible,'' I said, ''even if I gave you a clue.''

Ben brushed away the last remark as if a fly had been bothering him. He stopped and sat on the straw, tilting slightly to one side as if he was about to go to sleep, something he always did when working on a problem. There was a long silence.

''Does it have black ears?''he demanded suddenly.

I had no chance to answer for he followed with another question.

''Or eat snowflakes?''

''No.''

''Or gobble turnips?''

''Be serious,'' I said, getting serious myself.

''Does it swim backwards in puddings?''

I burst out laughing.

Ben jumped into the air waving a claw and shouting, ''I've got it. It's a three-legged erriwig.''

I fell back astonished for he had read my mind.

Ben was always more patronising when he summed up the moral of his lessons. ''This is a simple case of not-think, just play really but we have to start somewhere.''

I sat in silence.

''I can see you don't believe me or can't follow my thought. I assure you this is no magic. It is a science. I work only from what I notice and not-think, a most exact science, make no mistake.''

Once again the old doubts rushed through me. I imagined alternately that I had been tricked in some devious way, or I was really in the presence of a master detective. A detective who could not only disappear at will but read my mind. How it was done I could not tell. I could no longer doubt the value of his methods, for seeing was believing; but there were still nagging questions. Did he have other visitors? Where did he go after breakfast? Was I staying there by choice? I fussed over these doubts secretly. I even imagined in my worst mood that Ben was off the tracks and I was in danger of following him. It was the way he turned ordinary things upside down, not that ordinary things change, but Ben had a way of looking at things which made you rediscover them. Perhaps that is why he had no immediate memory, for everything was new to him, even the day. Where I would see a tree root burst through the wall, he would see strength. Where I saw only shadows, he would see the light that chased them.

Once, and only once, I put my misgivings into words and Ben replied, ''Cracked? Of course I'm cracked. It lets in the brightness.''

There were set lessons for everything, even down to what a detective should say to calm an angry queen bee. There were lessons on identifying prints, distinguishing emotions in plantigrade smells, unarmed combat, cracking nuts, learning bird songs and other calls, preserving smells, shadowing suspects, and many other subjects all illustrated by his colourful and amusing casebook which I have recorded elsewhere. Though this gave me much to think about and even more to practise, I grew resentful at being caged like an animal and forbidden to leave the chamber. I wanted to follow Ben through the skewer tunnel and discover what he did each day. I knew I would have to be cunning to outwit Ben, and decided to wait until I could sit stone more or less at will.

I waited my time and one day I took my chance.

* * * * *

We sat in munching silence over breakfast. Ben finished before me like he always did, licked his claws clean and started his wash and groom. He brushed his fur both ways around his face to get out the sleepy dust; he spat into his claws and scratched, with tiny quick movements, his back, underparts and under his foreclaws. He rubbed each of his nails on the stone he kept under the table and then announced he was ready to go. He never said goodbye but darted on all fours across the floor, slamming the door behind him.

This was my moment, the moment I was going to shadow him.

I counted to seventy-eight before I left the table. I was going to be as molelike as I could for I remembered his advice on shadowing: "If you are trailing a hedgehog, be a hedgehog; if a weasel, be a weasel." A suspect is listening for strange sounds, not familiar ones. If the office entrance had been too small, now I slipped easily into the skewer tunnel. I closed the door slowly, putting myself in the crack to screen off any light from the rocks. It was as dark as a fox's mouth. I was able to crouch comfortably on all fours though it was a tight fit. I sniffed the darkness hoping to detect any tell-tale air currents. There was a slight airwash as if a moth had fluttered past me leaving a faint wake of ripples. This was the normal breeze. I closed the door, lingering for a moment to feel my hair creeping in anticipation. I swam into the tunnel.

I crawled like a newt out of water taking deep gulps of air and stopping frequently to get used to the strange world I found myself in. I was on level ground. I could feel the tunnel sides around me not pressing in to squeeze me, but leaving just enough space to be guided by their smooth sides. I crawled faster, beginning to enjoy the ease I found in negotiating the straights and corners. I pushed with my feet and steered with my hands. If anything the draught was stronger, without a trace of that stale cloying atmosphere of a disused run. There was a freshness in the air, an indefinable scent which I found pleasing.

There was no light to see by so I fell headlong when the floor shelved steeply and suddenly. I jammed my legs into the sides but it did no good. I flew like a pea in a blow pipe. I was too frightened to breathe. I kept my hands upturned in front of my face. I closed my eyes expecting every corner to be my last. The darkness whistled past me, my hair blown back like streamers. Instead of crumbling at the end the bottom curved gently uphill and I halted, if not gracefully, still in one piece with my head and hands pointing in the right direction.

I counted to twenty and opened my eyes.

I noticed with a combination of excitement, indifference and mounting horror, that the darkness was framed by a thin band of light. It was in the shape of a square and shining through the cracks of a doorway. A strong draught was blowing in my face and there were sounds too. I wanted to turn back and crawl up the helter skelter. I wanted even more to know what was behind the door.

I crept nearer shielding my eyes from the light. I stretched out one hand and touched a hard surface rippled with rough edges. I closed my eyes to be sensitive to the sounds. They were coming more strongly. I listened to them, frail and whining, coming in torrents continuous as the wind catching frozen netting. I thought I heard the fastness of a pine wood or a tree bowed down with ice. I was not born to be courageous and would never have entered the doorway had not the breeze brought a more familiar sound, the sound of someone singing. The smile creased my face as I recognised the high squeaking voice, alternating with green rushes of music, then drawn out with grave gravelly notes, as thin as any wire. It was Ben.

I remember the song for I often sing it to myself. I call it *Love Song*.

> Your eyes are the finest eyes I see
> The water's edge is the clearest place to be

And to see your eyes
There's not a place
Where your eyes can't be.

Your face is the finest face I know
The pebbles they glisten in the frost
And to see your face
There's not a place
Where your face can't be.

Your touch is the warmest touch I know
The sun it rises on my face
And to feel your touch
There's not a place
Where your touch can't be

Your love for the garden makes it grow
Your face and eyes both see the dreams I know
And to find your love, there's not a place
Where your love can't grow
And to find your love, there's not a place
Where your love can't grow.

I listened to the song until it vanished under the distant stream of sounds. My heart beat wildly and my hand toyed with the door, still uncertain in my mind which way to go. I listened as Ben had taught me, trying to pick out the details of the sounds, unravel them one by one. There was something more familiar about the details, as if the sounds had been distorted, stretched out in some way. The more I listened the more I recognised the straining of roots against wind and soil, the rubbing of ingrowing branches, common enough in old thorn trees. The sounds were so familiar I was sure that once past the doorway I would not find the stained glass world of my imagination, but an underground chamber close to the surface, and a hole where daytime sounds entered.

I pulled open the door and breathed deeply. There was an unexpected earthiness in the air, a sweet mustiness I knew so well but had not tasted for a while. I sat stone as best I could in my excitement, the top part of me hovering between the cold grey earth, the underparts of me staying as a boy. A brilliant shaft of light lit the chamber, pokey by comparison to the office, and full of shadows where the light crossed tree roots. I saw a mound of roots and earth with a great stone slab on top.

I heard the sounds clearly now, winter sounds of the Downs, but magnified and altered by the resonance in the chamber. I still did not recognise the chamber. I looked carefully into the corners where the light reached. I could see something else glinting, a weak thin light, which did not come from the crack in the ceiling but from under the rubble. At the same time I picked out another sound as if something was being dragged from one place to another. I looked back at the light and wondered what it could be. Again I heard the sound of something being dragged across the floor. It came from the other side of the mound. Something was breathing heavily, grunting and groaning as if pulling a heavy weight.

I reappeared by the doorway and crept forward. A strange familiarity crept over me. My body tingled with it. I stayed in the shadows well clear of the shaft of light. There was something so familiar about the roots and the smoothness of the tunnel side I was leaning against. I could not find the words to match the feeling. The atmosphere became oppressive. I noticed with fascination and horror that the glinting light was half buried under the rubble. The glint I saw was not the light, but a reflection of a metal object. The grunting and groaning continued. It came from the other side of the mound of rocks and roots. I could hear scratching sounds and heavy mutterings, and a rock being pulled clear of the mound. I must have made a sound for the grunting stopped and a bad-tempered voice squeaked, ''Who's there?''

I sat stone concentrating on the rubble around me. On the far side of the mound, from behind a boulder, appeared a sharp pointed snout covered with dust.

''Who's that?'' squeaked Ben. He sightwhiskered the light and gloom before disappearing behind the rocks. Once more I listened to his sighs as he tugged some heavy rocks. I retreated as qietly as possible. I found the bark door and hurried back with a swarm of thoughts buzzing inside me.

Chapter Six

I did not stop or once look back down the helter skelter of passageways until I reached Ben's office. Then I collapsed by the table heaving to catch my breath and quieten my thoughts. Though I had no doubt the capstone chamber was the one I had entered that fateful day—had I not seen what looked like my lamp?—there was something odd and puzzling, something which didn't fit my recollections, like a stone in a shoe which hurts but you can't find it. Why had I not recognised it first of all? Why was it bigger than I remembered it? I had often noticed how objects in Ben's world could be very big, then smaller the next time I saw them. Ben was not always the same size. When we first met he was a fraction of my size; lately we were looking each other in the eyes. To say the least I was baffled.

There was something else too. It was the lamp. I could not be sure whether I had seen a reflection from the light or whether the lamp still glowed. The one thing which could have given a sense of time had proved a puzzle. I thought I was losing my mind.

I would have thought stranger things had not the tunnel door burst open and a dark pointed shape sped across the floor to the table.

Ben was a creature of habit if nothing else. He brushed the dust off himself and placed a pile of wriggling worms on the table. There were always twenty but he counted them one by one just to make sure. Then, without a word to me, he guzzled them one by one until they were gone. He brushed his whiskers.

"Nothing like dinner," he squeaked contentedly.

I greeted him coldly as for once I thought I could see

through his games with me. Though I was frightened if he should discover my disobedience, I was pleased to have the upper hand. I wondered how he would lie to my questions.

"Many worms?" I asked, knowing full well the boring answer.

He counted his claws. "Twenty."

There was silence.

"Can I ask you a question?"

Ben grunted.

"Why do you always leave here so clean and come back so dusty?"

"And why are you so nosy?" he snapped back.

"Well I was just thinking . . ."

"Well don't."

We sat opposite each other in silence. Ben pretended to be dozing though I could see he was sightwhiskering me carefully. I tried once more.

"Why are your nails so sharp when you leave and so blunted when you return?"

Ben leaned on the table. He glared angrily at me. "I've told you not to ask me those questions."

"Well I will," I shouted back with spirit.

Ben stepped back one pace with a look of astonishment.

I could not stop myself now. "I'm fed up with being cooped in this cage. I can't stand it any more." I stamped my feet.

Ben banged the table with his claw. "You will do what I say."

"I won't," I shouted. I stamped my feet again.

"You will," he shouted even louder.

"I *won't*, and anyway it's too late."

"Too late?" he said, his voice suddenly becoming softer. "Too late for what?"

It was the time for plain speaking. "I followed you today."

I don't know what I expected, if anything, but I was shocked by what happened. Ben flung his claws in the air and waved them wildly. He jumped up and down. He swayed on his hind claws. He kicked the straw into the air, all the time whistling through his teeth a shrill, threadbare music. He banged his claws on the table and danced what looked like a jig in front of me. Then, as suddenly as it had begun, he flopped onto the straw beside me and looked into my eyes, his whiskers quivering on end.

"Excellent . . . excellent," he said between his heavy panting. "And to think I didn't even see you. You have come a long way."

"But . . . but," I stammered, "I was forbidden to go into the tunnel."

"Exactly."

"You told me not to go and I went."

"Exactly."

I moved around uneasily. "You're not angry?"

"Angry? I'm delighted."

I was speechless.

He stood on his hind claws placing his foreclaws across his furry chest. "You see, Fellman, you are not the only one to be deceived. I have tricked you but believe me it is for a good reason. I would be failing in my duties if I let you join me before you are ready. As I said, out there are many dangers. Unless you could deceive me, what chance would you have? Now is not the time to say everything, you will see soon enough, but I had to be sure you were ready to come if we were called."

My mind shook with questions.

"That is why I tricked you. I knew you would be ready when you had learned to deceive and disobey me."

"It was all planned," I said weakly.

"I'm afraid so, but I had to know whether you listened to me like a puppet or had a mind of your own. Then, and only then, would I know you were ready."

"Ready for what?" I couldn't help asking.

"The last lesson."

*   *   *   *   *

"The secret of not-think," began Ben grandly with extravagant sweeps of his claws, "is older than the thorns of this valley. It has been passed in our family for many generations but I fear I am the last of the great mole detectives."

He paused to make sure I had appreciated the fact.

"It is the secret, the final solution that many have sought, and that," he smilecreased mischievously, "is why they have never found it. We have a story in our family that not-think was discovered by my great-great-great-great-grandmole Wormhole (Wormhole the First for short) when he accidentally tripped over a root and banged his snout on a stone. When he recovered he saw everything differently, gave up his rich greensand tunnels, and came to these bare hills where he lived as a hermit, that is, until he started the detective business. He was loved by all those who met him, and the methods he devised have continued ever since, a tradition unbroken from master to apprentice and so forth. Many have tried to imitate our methods but have failed, for only not-think can penetrate the farthest corners of our minds. Not-think is the unknown. It is practical. Anyone can master it instantly, for in not-think there is nothing to learn." He began to laugh, a silly shrill laugh.

I shifted uneasily.

Ben thrust his claws by his sides and walked up and down by the table, addressing the darkness around us. The light flashed across the wall behind him.

"Let me give you an example," he said. "Imagine you are excited for some reason and it is my task to discover what it is. I might use the art of noticing and discover that your hands twitch differently according to your moods."

I nodded in agreement.

"I might see they twitch fast with wonder, slowly when

thinking, sideways when moody, or not at all as now, when you are thinking too hard.''

I put my hands under the table.

''Or, for example,'' continued Ben in his monotonous patronising voice, while still pacing up and down in front of me, ''I might notice your breathing. The way it gets shorter when you are frightened or mystified, or deeper when you are relaxed and sleepy, or the way you hold your breath, as now, when you are thinking too hard.''

I breathed deeply in and out to confuse him.

''So I see this and one hundred other little things and still do not know the answer. What am I to do? Guess?''

I knew the right answer was no. I shook my head.

''Exactly. Guessing is no science. Only the inferior mice detectives guess. I have looked as much as I can look, smelt as much as I can smell, touched as much as I can touch, thought as much as I can think and still I do not know. I am up against darkness, as thick as any yewshade. Then, and only then, do I turn to not-think.''

''You must think me thistle-brained,'' I butted in, ''but how can you think if you are not thinking?''

Ben shuffled up to me, so close I could feel his warm breath. He stopped to take something from under the table by his bed. It was a shell. He tapped it gently on his claw.

''Can you see it?'' he asked. ''It is something very special.''

I looked closely but could only see the pad of his claws and the tufts of velvety fur around the nails.

''I can see nothing,'' I said, suspecting that he was making a fool of me.

''Look harder. It's there, something very special.'' He held his claws even nearer to my face.

I ran my eyes over every part of his claw but could still see nothing. I told him so.

''Give up?'' he said.

''Yes.''

With his spare foreclaw, he very carefully picked out something. He held it up to me.

''That,'' he said smilecreasing, ''is something very very special.''

"I can't see anything," I said.

"Of course you can't. Because this," he held it to my eyes, "is the smallest thing in the world and that's why nobody can see it." He returned it carefully into the shell and put it back under the table.

He continued pacing up and down in front of the table. "That," he sighed drawing out the words in one breath, "is simplicity herself. But who can see her? She is small like worms, bees and wood crawlies. She is shy and nameless, and when something is small, shy and nameless it is hard to see. The point is, when I not-think, I think to find out not what I know but what I don't know. So if I know what I not-think, which I don't, I would not need to think at all. Follow?"

I said nothing.

"This is the way of not-think, to be small and find out what is not there."

"But," I said, "if it's not there, where is it?"

"Ah ha," he squeaked delightedly, kicking a flurry of straw into the air and banging his tail with excitement, "you have to ask the right questions—and then forget them."

He clutched his sides and started tottering on his claws as he burst into laughter. "Hahahaha it's so easy . . . so easy hahaha . . ."

I finally lost my temper with this childish, indulgent display. I banged the table loudly and when I had his attention I told him I had had enough of his crackpot theories.

"How do I know it's so easy? A bogus yarn like the spiders spin. If it's so easy," I persisted, "tell me what is on my mind."

I had a longing to cut Ben to size and I had a way to do it. I knew Ben was cleverer than I thought he was, but not even a master detective could describe something he had never seen. I fingered the old bone square with the strange markings which I kept in my pocket. I had him now I thought.

Ben grunted in the affirmative and shuffled in his awkward way in a large circle around me and the table. His stooping figure occasionally caught the flash of the rock lights. It reminded me of a pathetic old man, but there was still something of his arrogant manner, particularly the way he would not bother to look at me when speaking, talking instead to the darkness above our heads.

"Do bluebottles go on holiday?"

I had learnt enough not to answer these absurd questions. He had stopped and was gazing into the flickering lights.

"Do worms like piggy backs?" he asked in the same quizzing voice.

I kept my pleasure secret for he was so far from the truth. I watched him certain that he would give up or be forced to guess desperately. He left the rock lights and shuffled against the background of shadows around the table.

If I had any feelings of remorse that I had tricked him with my impossible thought, I did not regret my desire to knock the stuffing and superiority out of my master. He gazed up at the ceiling.

"Do stars have night caps?" he squeaked.

"*No no no,*" I said delightedly.

His manner changed abruptly. His whiskers fell and he dropped on all fours, staring at me with an open-mouthed look of amazement and the nearest thing to disbelief creeping across his furfolds.

I felt embarrassed as if I had upset him. I could see none of his arrogance and contempt. He crawled towards me, a shadow of himself, wobbling on his claws so he could not keep a straight course.

He did not speak when he reached the table opposite myself. He leaned against the side, a crumpled mole. He rocked to and fro, and what I had mistaken to be sadness of some kind, I recognised as a state of high excitement. His fur quivered. His whiskers quivered, as did his tail which was so numbed with excitement it could hardly move. He gripped the side of the table, and looking at me with trembling whiskers, he whispered, "You have seen it."

"Seen what?"

"The . . . the map."

"Map? What map?" I wondered what he was talking about.

"The map, the map," he repeated feverishly. "Where is it?"

"Where's what?"

"The map, the map. Where is it?"

I had no chance to answer. At that moment there was a dull hammering at the tunnel door, the main entrance where Ben kept his sign. We both heard the rasping of low snortling tongues, the sound of claws scratching the earth and a steady beating as if it was hailing pigeon eggs. We were not expecting visitors.

"Who can it be?" I asked. Whoever it was beat louder at the tunnel door.

BANG. BANG. BANG.

"*Go away*," squeaked Ben furiously banging his claws at the sound.

BANG. BANG. BANG.

Ben shook his claws at the door. "I'll teach them to come here without an appointment." He shot on all fours across the straw to the skewer tunnel. The door slammed. It reopened almost immediately. Ben reappeared with a skewer in either claw. He shuffled across the floor and waited by the shadow near the door.

BANG. BANG. BANG. The hammering stopped.

"Come in," said Ben.

The door opened slowly. The light from the nearest rocks cast a large wedge-shaped shadow on the wall. It had a long pointed snout that couldn't keep still.

Ben raised the skewers above his head.

I was horrified by what might happen, but I need not have worried. The visitors were far too cautious. No sooner had the shadow appeared than it withdrew to be replaced by anxious sniffing sounds and a single voice, a voice which droned like an old steam kettle on a steady heat.

"Wes hale," it greeted us.

There was no reply.

"We have come with a message for Ben of Thorngrove."

"Who from?" said Ben sharply, though he lowered the skewers a little.

"From Burley Pickles, the badger of the Four Ways. He has sent us."

There was a long silence broken by a curse.

"Toads' bellies," moaned Ben flinging down the

60

skewers, "can't I have a bit of peace?" He paused. "I suppose you had better come in."

The shadow of the long-pointed snout appeared again on the wall. It crept into the office scraping its belly on the straw, worrying the ground with its constant sniffing and turning of its restless body. Its long scaly tail thudded with the steady beat of a skipping rope. A second, a third, and a fourth entered in single file sending their shadows dancing hugely around the walls. They fanned the air with their whiskers, squeaking and whimpering to themselves, following their leader through the gloom and into the centre of the room. I smelt the mustiness before they reached the table, the unmistakable presence of rats.

Ben slammed the door and followed after them muttering to himself. He showed no sign of remembering our conversation, in fact by the time he reached the table he had become his cheerful self now that he was thinking of his friend Pickles.

I could not say the same for myself. Though I had chased and once caught a rat in a barn, it was a different matter meeting one underground. I was so close I could see their white underparts. I kept a low profile half-buried in the straw behind where Ben was sitting and talking to the leader. The rats equally regarded me with suspicion, and it was only when Ben, fed up with our constant furtive glances at each other, shouted: "Don't worry. It's only people and eats sausages," that I emerged from my hiding place. I joined Ben by his side.

The largest rat was telling Ben that they had come to escort us to Burley Pickles who lived on the crossroads, the other side of Ram's Hill. They would sleep while we got ready but had an order to return as soon as possible. They would not say what the reason was but only that Burley Pickles had said he was expecting a visitor. An important visitor. He said that Ben would understand. If he did, he showed no sign of it. He ordered the rats into the shadows and then sat for a long while playing with his whiskers.

I sat counting my thoughts too. I had forebodings that nothing would ever be the same. How young I was and still so far from the sound breaking! I could not see how the pieces were fitting together. I was aware of the tension in the air but not of its meaning. How could I know that whichever way I turned it would be the right way? That however strange, adverse or ill-fated my circumstances, the thread would be gathered and spun, stretched and completed, with colours and patterns my mind could never entertain. When the wool was being spun I could see only approaching chaos, a mole rushing by or a man waiting for the sky to fall to catch larks. I saw only a little boy lost. Now I see differently.

I thought Ben had fallen asleep. His foreclaws were stretched across the table and he was snoring with every second breath. I looked closer and saw that his whiskers were still bristling, a sure sign that he was thinking deeply.

Suddenly his claws clattered on the table and he sat upright as bright as a cherry. ''Where was I?'' he squeaked cheerfully. He did not wait for an answer, not that he expected one, but carried on talking.

''I have been doing a little not-think,'' he said, ''and I do believe it is time for me to go. Pickles is the last badger to make a fuss of things so it must be something important.''

''What about me?'' I said with a sinking feeling inside.

''What about you?''

''Well, can't I come?

He scratched his fur one way, he scratched it the other way.

''Mmmmmmmmm yes, but you'll have to pass a test.''

I agreed readily as I had no wish as yet for a desk job.

I wondered what it would be. I tried to remember what a lame earwig's trail looks like, or how to preserve the smell of a summer's night, or to count the drops of water in a puddle. I tried to remember some sign words of hedgerow mime, the language used by spiders and other crawlies. I counted the number of things a detective had to forget if he was to not-think and how I would knock out a fox if he attacked me. My mind hurtled at ever increasing speed down these ever narrowing tracks. I grew dizzy. I thought I was going to faint.

I fainted.

"Good," I could hear Ben saying cheerfully, "be sure not to bring any luggage."

I sat up and rubbed my eyes. "What about the test?" I asked.

"Test? Why you have had it already."

"Have I?"

"Yes. And you passed easily."

"What was it?" I could not help asking.

Ben sighed a paternal sigh. "Any fool, even a one-legged cross-eyed millepede can take a test. All you have to do is to get a grip on yourself." He gripped the edge of the table and contorted his face into a horribly grim, determined look. He let go and smilecreased.

"The very thought of a test would make any superior detective want to faint. Thinking, thinking, thinking and not one sign of a crack."

He sightwhiskered me. "Yes Fellman, I think you are beginning to crack up nicely."

I said nothing until I remembered there was something about going on a journey.

"How long will we be gone?" I asked.

"Oh I should think as long as it takes."

"Takes what?"

"Takes to wait and see."

*   *   *   *   *

"Dear, dear me." Ben took another anxious look around the office. "Have I forgotten anything?"

It seemed ages since Ben had announced that we would leave that instant. Ages later he was still fussing and scurrying among any corners that may have hidden something, searching for things to pack into his detective travelling bag, a small leather pouch. I noticed that it looked remarkably similar in design to my own. He filled it with spare and extra spare bundles of dried worms, several shellboxes with lids, a piece of thick glass for magnifying things, some chalk and two truffles. He strapped it round his middle with twined straws. He stood on two claws and puffed out his chest. If there was a mirror, I thought, he would have admired himself in it. As it is he enjoyed flexing his broad digging shoulders, and running his claws through each other as if to feel, time and time again, how sharp they were. He spat in his claws and groomed himself thoroughly, then returned to the business of looking for last minute things.

I often wondered whether moles naturally had untidy minds, as Ben was incapable of remembering anything, for no sooner had he put something down than he would have lost it. Finally he announced he was packed and he expected everyone to jump to attention. He woke the rats roughly, kicking the straw into their faces. He lined us in a row and strutted up and down in front of us.

"I shall be leading," he said pompously, with his claws thrust behind his back. "I know a short cut which will get us there by owlight. Any questions?"

"Sir," said a small voice with a loudly banging tail, "can we eat first?"

Other tails banged in agreement.

"And what will you eat?" quizzed Ben. "My store is empty. The sooner we get to Pickles' the sooner we shall eat."

I knew Ben was lying but I mentioned this episode to show that though he had a mind as broad as the Downs, he could be petty and deceitful when it suited him.

To my surprise and misgiving, we did not leave by the main entrance or the skewer tunnel but crawled to end of the cavern I had explored before. I was uneasy about our escort, not that I thought they meant us any harm, but that we should have one at all. We set off as a group straggling abreast of each other until we reached the bright lights of the rocks, even brighter because of the darkness beyond.

The leading rats had stopped, straining on their hind paws to search the darkness and the tunnel Ben had promised. We all stopped.

"What is it?" squeaked Ben irritably.

"The path," said a mystified voice, its tail skipping on the floor, "we can't find it."

"Gone?" snorted Ben. "Impossible."

While the rats sniffed in an ever increasing circle, Ben shot on all fours into the darkness. We heard him tapping the sides as if looking for a hollow. A squeaking sound set my teeth on edge. It was followed by a door slamming.

"Ah here we are." A dark, pointed shape appeared before us. "Just as I said it would be." He glanced at the leading rats, then back to me. "It's a good job my wits were not out woolgathering."

"They're going to be nothing but trouble," whispered Ben when I reached his side. He had his claw on an ancient looking door covered with cobwebs and lichen, and in damp corners by large sprouting ferns. The door squeaked when it opened, and a breeze washed our faces with a dry rotty flavour which clung to our bodies like horseflies.

"Well what do you expect?" said Ben. "It hasn't been used for a while that's all. This hill is honeycombed with tunnels. They were once all part of our family estate.'' He looked at our anxious faces. ''It's safe and dry, I promise you. We will be at Pickles' by owlight.''

The rats were not impressed and continued searching the breeze for threatening scents. In the end they would enter the tunnel only if Ben and I took the lead and they brought up the rear.

Ben paddled into the darkness thumping his tail on the ceiling to keep his bearings and sometimes stopping so suddenly to sightwhisker that I bumped into him. This happened so often that he began to lose his temper, especially as most of the clearing work fell to him. It was difficult going. The tunnel had not been used in years for the grass roots hung like thick cobwebs and these had to be cut and trampled down before we could pass. Occasionally we were brought to a standstill by a jungle of thick taproots; then we would take it in turns to cut through them, a nasty job as they tasted bitter with sap. Apart from these obstacles, I found I squeezed easily through the tunnel, except at corners or where it shelved too deeply to pass under a block of flint or stone. Only once did the rats have to dig to widen the way, but even that was not serious.

Later on the tunnel sides became smooth as they cut through the white chalk. There were no roots to tickle our faces and we made good distance. It seemed to me that we kept pace with the echoes which continually bounced off the tunnel sides in front of us. It got slower when the passageway rose steeply to straddle close to the earthline, to twist and ferret among ancient tree roots, to dip under a winterbourne and skirt large stones.

"We mustn't be late," muttered Ben to himself each time scrambling more feverishly through the tunnel.

The rats heaved and grunted behind us to keep up with Ben's pace; but they never complained. I knew we were in a winter tunnel now, a deep tunnel, for only far below can the worms be found when the surface is hard and cold. We were too far down for grass roots. We sped along the tunnel as fast as a racing vole until Ben stopped suddenly to sniff telltale breaks in the breeze.

"It's a hollow," he whispered.

We crawled slowly forwards.

"There it is," said Ben with a trace of excitement in his voice. "It's an entrance to a summer tunnel."

I looked up and saw a mass of tiny roots in what was once a tunnel. It smelt musty but not as musty as ours.

Ben was reluctant to leave. He fanned his whiskers and snorted as if he was sighing. How inadequate it is to describe squeaks and sniffles and snorts. If Ben was a person I would say he had been struck by a recollection too painful. He crouched on the tunnel floor. We all crouched. He spoke softly, almost forgetting we were there.

"I was two summers old then. Grandmole Wernte had let me explore the tunnels. I loved exploring the tunnels. I would spend all day in them but I had to go back to sleep and have lessons. He always told me not to go too far, but I always did."

Ben looked up at the summer run.

"I found this tunnel when I was two. I wondered where it went. I always did what I shouldn't do. I explored. I came to a meadow covered with water which sparkled. I could not stop. The sun had not come up. I explored."

He sighed again. He got up and spoke into the tunnel, his voice broken with feeling.

> She
> teeny tiny flitter mice
> heaven loves
> the erriwig, roots from grass

dew glittering
no time always
slugs sparkle, cherry fall pink.
Thornblossoms. Ah
Cowpie ooops, sky warbling
baa baa sheep I never told
Whoops! silk soft sweet
She
More no tell
together bee buzz cowslip
together ah She
honeywarm
together.

Ben sank back onto the floor of the tunnel.

"Fellman?"

"Yes?"

"If it hurts remembering, is that crying?"

"Sometimes," I said.

There was a long pause. "Then I must be crying. It hurts."

Silence. The rats shuffled behind me.

"Another thing."

"Yes?"

"Will it ever stop?"

"Yes," I said. "You will forget it."

"Memory snap?"

"Yes, memory snap."

There was another long pause.

"Then I never want to forget."

Ben must have remembered for at least ten feet, for we were that distance from the summer tunnel when he passed without seeing a worm dangling from the roof.

*   *   *   *   *

The going was easier and faster now. We had left the trees and their roots behind and were slipping and sliding under a hill. I could almost imagine the pasture a few inches above our heads, the larks above that and the clouds highest of all sailing over the Downs. We were travelling headfirst, just below the earthline where there were fewer roots and the ground was still soft enough for the tunnel to be large and airy. How far we shuffled following our tireless furry leader I do not know, how long I cannot tell. The rats heaved and grunted behind me but they never complained. Perhaps they thought as I did, the quicker we moved the sooner we arrived.

When Ben did slam on the brakes, jamming his claws into the sides so the screechings drummed in my ears, it was too late to stop. We were going too fast. We hit each other like falling dominoes, a sprawling mass of bodies, tails and whiskers. We jammed the tunnel and Ben was at the bottom of it all.

''Toads' bellies,'' he cursed. He breast-stroked frantically to free himself, and when he had done so he gouged the earth from the tunnel side. He flung it so it landed with an ominous whack against something hard and solid. Even I could feel that the breeze had gone and in its place was the returning pressure of our own hectic movements.

The tunnel was blocked.

Ben looked as if he were going to throw a fit. His shoulder fur rippled as he wrung his claws.

''It's a stake, a damned stake.'' He gouged more earth from the side and flung it into the darkness so it thudded against something hard. He crawled forward and banged it, so the rattle of his claws echoed angrily in that confined space. Then he hit the floor, the sides, the ceiling and the floor again. His squealings got louder and louder. I joined the rats which were retreating a little farther back. Ben raged in the darkness. He clawed the earth and steamed until the earth clung to him.

As I have said moles suffer from memory snap, for no sooner had he rested and panted to get his breath than he got up as if nothing had happened. He wiped the sweat from his brow and ran his claws through his fur to pick out the dirt. He crawled forward and tapped the stake, this time softly. He tapped it again all round until he was sure how big it was. Then he half turned and said calmly, ''Watch this. You might have to do it sometime.''

He braced his hind claws against the side, and, leaning on

one paw, he tore at the opposite wall. He did not use neat and fussy strokes, but worked with a wild fury that scattered the earth over our heads. We retreated. He snorted loudly when he rested to catch his breath, sometimes lunging back with a claw to stop the earth piling on his tail. His back arched in time to his claws, springing backwards and forwards as he gouged wider the opening by the stake. He worked like this for a while, then he turned over to use his other claw. His body shuddered with the effort. The rats made themselves busy spreading the soil thinly down the tunnel. With a final snort Ben disappeared. He had reached the other side of the stake.

The airwash flapped in our faces like a cold flannel. We waited in the darkness for Ben to recover his strength before leaving in single file, this time with two rats leading and two rats behind us. We travelled cautiously, stopping more often to sightwhisker the darkness and listen for the smallest change in the air pressure. I knew something was wrong and so did the others. We were more alert, tense, afraid of the echoes of our own movements. More than once Ben urged the rats to go faster for they crept forward no quicker than a snail.

There was no mistaking the sound. We heard it when we crawled round a corner.

"Stop," squeaked Ben, but we did not need his encouragement.

A dull resonant sound echoed down the tunnel as if the earth was being hammered steadily, relentlessly. It got louder. The tunnel magnified the sounds. There were other sounds too, of skipping tails and half supressed whimperings.

"Quiet," said Ben. He sightwhiskered the darkness but even the master detective could not decipher the echoes. They had never heard the sound of a man banging a stake. I told them what it was and that the banging would stop soon. It did.

The rats were all for digging out of the tunnel there and then, until Ben warned that there was only thin grassland above and hungry hoverhawks above that. They changed their minds.

I tried to reassure them.

"They are humans," I told them, speaking louder to help them understand. "They are banging stakes into the ground. They are not out to get us. If we travel quietly we will be safe." That helped, but not much. After that I led the way and that helped a little more.

I listened with my hands pressed against the tunnel sides for vibrations. I found a stake which had glanced through the side of the tunnel. There could be no doubt now that we had run into a fencing team. I had seen such men working around the greensand farms, especially at spring after the rain and frost had done its damage. I knew that they often worked in pairs and that by ill-luck our tunnel coincided with the line of the fence. I knew that once past them we would be safe. I told this again to the others and told them to make as little sound as possible.

Sounds travel easily in the earth and so do voices, for soon I heard a rough muffled conversation somewhere in the distance and above our heads.

I pulled myself along the tunnel hardly daring to breathe. The others followed me silently, though when the voices became louder some of the rats started to whimper. We were close to them now, how near I could not tell, but near enough to feel the shock of a stake falling to the ground, and an angry curse following it. I did not stop for if I had I would have lost my nerve. I kept going hoping that the others had kept going too. I had been feeling my way carefully in the darkness, having no longer Ben's stumpy tail to guide me, when something hard hit the turf in front, almost above my head.

A stake had come through the tunnel roof. It was pulled out almost as quickly. The brightness flooded the tunnel.

"There's that bloody rabbit run again," said a voice.

I crouched back into the darkness along with the others, shielding the light from my eyes. It entered through the shaft left by the stake a few feet away.

The rats started whining.

"Sssssh," breathed Ben through clenched teeth.

"What shall we do?" said the voice.

"Ah just dig it to one side," said another.

The rats continued whining. Their tails skipped even faster.

"What was that?" said a voice.

"What, Joe?"

"Listen. There's a bloody rat down there."

There was silence, except for the rats whining, their tails skipping.

"I told you didn't I. It's a bloody rat. A nest by the sound of it. And tuppence a tail is a jug of ale, isn't it? Give us that fork."

There was the sound of something heavy being picked up.

My mind worked quickly. I turned to the others and told them to run with me. I did not run back into the tunnel but forwards and under the bright light breaking through the hole. I scratched at the sides and kicked with my feet for extra speed. I clawed my way into the darkness. I clawed my way past roots, past stones. I did not look back. I did not look forward. The earth flew behind me. I let the darkness swallow me up. I heard the fork like a hammer blow.

"Faster faster," squealed voices behind me.

I had a glimpse of dark pointed bodies speeding across the light threshhold, their bodies clear one moment, the next not there. I heard scurryings and whinings in the distance.

There was a terrific crash in the roof behind me as splinters of light, briefly, shot through the tunnel. I clawed my way under the roots which lined the tunnel roof. I was in darkness. I was panting.

"Blast," cried a man, "it's gone under the hedge." His footsteps faded away.

I saw the fork crashing through the roof just missing skewering a rat following Ben.

They did not stop when they reached me.

"Carry on, carry on," said Ben wildly.

We left the tangled thick roots and followed the tunnel which twisted and shelved between them. We did not stop until the tunnel dipped under a large flint and where water had washed away a hollow. I could not hear any voices but I could still hear the fork lancing the turf and tunnelways farther back. We listened for the footfalls of our escort, but it was the rat, with sharper hearing, which picked out the sound first. It was a weak scratching noise, with frequent gaps of silence as if something was dragging a heavy weight then resting. For a while the scratching sounds got louder, then softer, and as it got softer the silences grew longer. There were no more scratching sounds. The tunnel was silent. We waited for as long as we could, then Ben, assuming command, ordered us to continue. There were no tears, a moment's silence perhaps, but once out of sight and back into the journey, my companions were their normal selves.

Many times I have tried to understand this. It is not that they feel nothing, in my experience they are very aware of life, but they do not cling to it like ourselves. At heart they are practical. Death is always in the hedgerow, lying in wait on the branches, concealed in the grass. It is the one thing which is certain in their lives. That is why they never remember, to protect themselves from the pain that always hurt me.

As Ben once said on the subject: "Why worry about your shadow? Only flies do that."

*   *   *   *   *

I stayed in my thoughts the rest of the journey. I stayed at the rear, leaving the rat and Ben to cut through the rough patches. I was sick with questions, or were they imaginings? Who was Pickles? Why were we going there? I was even homesick for Ben's office and its flickering world of shadows; at least the familiar, however strange, is a comfort.

I had not seen the outside world, the world of humans, for so long. What was real? I was also puzzled by an indefinable feeling that Ben not only spoke to me as his apprentice, but as if, how can I say it, I was one of his kind. Me a mole? I pinched myself when these thoughts came and would rub my hands and face for any sign of fur, whiskers or a wet nose. But even this behaviour struck me as a sign of my sickness. It just isn't normal to imagine you are a mole.

The light took us all by surprise. We had been crawling steadily along a straight stretch but there were so many roots it was impossible to see far into the gloom. Then the tunnel turned sharply, and after we had cleared the cobwebs, we saw the sky at the end of a vertical shaft. There were spears of dun-coloured grass around the edges, and, instead of a blue sky, there was a smoky cloud cover, the sort one sees on damp days in the White Horse Vale.

"At last, at last," squeaked Ben delightedly, "The Four Ways. It won't be long now till supper."

I was the last to pull myself clear of the tunnel. It was so cold above ground I shivered, the sort of cold that creeps into you and breathes life into forgotten aches. The rat shivered but not Ben, he was too busy sightwhiskering the beeches by the edge of the crossroads ahead of us. I heard the coorroorooo and wingcrack of a pigeon but nothing else. There were no leaves on the trees to rustle, or sun to stain the light with small browns and greens. This was not what I was expecting. I wished I was back in the tunnel. The only sound I heard was the wind rattling the old cow parsley, and a thin piping among the winter branches.

Ben refused to be weighed down. "See that," he said brightly pointing with a claw across the track and at a quadrangle of chalk and redbrick farm buildings. "That's where Pickles lives."

The buildings fitted neatly into a corner of the crossroads. The beeches ran along one side of them, and where they ended, a ragged dark hedge took over. It disappeared on both sides of the trackway as far as I could see. I looked more closely. I smiled in recognition. We were on the Kingston Lisle-Lambourn road, and the hedgerow was the Ridgeway crossing in front of us. To think that Kingston was only a mile down the road. We were on a grass verge opposite the farm buildings, and by the edge of a quarry. I looked across the quarry and saw the skeleton of Britchcombe Wood obscuring the skyline and straddling the lower slopes around Ram's Hill. I followed the line of the trees, half-shielding my eyes with my hand, for though it was cloudy it was bright as sunlight to me. I followed the landfall of the Downs where it slips easily into the greensand farms. I found it hard to see the view all at once. It was as big as my eyes and they were half-covered. I followed the fields beyond Combe Spring Wood and saw the green stubble of the sprouting winter barley. I saw the ivy twined around the trees, but when I looked for my father's farm near Fawler I could only see it dimly through the elms where the rooks nested. I was surprised to see how fat the sheep were on the permanent pastures until I saw that there were no lambs. I had difficulty recognising landmarks. I thought the dimness was in my eyes, then I saw that the dimness was also in the land. I saw it first by the damp meadows. They were covered by a veil of mist, so fine it was easy not to see it. When I did, I saw the same whiteness everywhere, evening autumn mist, except it wasn't autumn. The mist thickened in the approaching owlight, drifting gently over the meadows and among the sheep.

I turned away when our remaining rat left us. I watched him hop and pick his way through the grass, his grey back and white underparts blending so well that in moments he was out of sight.

"I think we'll cross here," said Ben, peering across the track which separated us from the farm buildings. He shuffled through the grass and was on the point of stepping into the road when he waved me to stop with his claw. He crouched and twisted his head so he could sightwhisker the sky in all directions. Eventually he stopped, looking in the direction of Britchcombe Wood. I could see the wood clearly and the sky through it, for there were no leaves. I looked across the fields where the barley pierced the dull brown surface, and into the higher, steeper slopes full of sheep.

Ben whistled to me under his breath. I crouched in the long grass keeping one eye on the distant wood. The black outlines of the trees, some entwined with columns of ivy, were criss-crossed with patterns of mist. I wondered what Ben had heard until I heard the sound too. It came from beyond the wood, from one of the steep-sided valleys. It was a dark and half-formed sound, as the wind blows on a pine copse, whistling on the green needles, muffled by the closeness of the trees.

Britchcombe Wood grew darker round the edges.

There was no mistaking the darkness. It flapped like a sail in a high wind. It still came from beyond the wood but it filled the valleys and fields as well as our ears with its approaching thunder. A tide, a black mark, flooded

Britchcombe Wood. It was halfway up the trees, eating more of the sky, covering the tree tops, a rising black hill which was not a hill. It hovered on the skyline a moment. It sunk below the skyline. Britchcombe Wood reappeared, and so did the black outlines of the trees.

We listened to the thunder until we heard it no longer.

"Dear, oh dear," said Ben. He turned back towards the road. He sniffed deeply several times.

"I wonder if dinner's ready." He bent the strawlike grasses and stepped for the second time into the road. "Whatever you do," he called back, "don't step on the goosegrass, the seeds are a curse if they stick on your tail."

It took a long time crossing the road, especially climbing in and out of the three ruts. I never realised they were so big and I was glad they were not filled with water.

The nearer we got to the corner of the building and the white field gate, the lighter grew Ben's step. Instead of dragging his claws as if they were dead weights as he usually did, he picked them up as if he was skipping and sung in his crackling bell-pitch voice an old song. I think it was one of grandmole Wernte's.

> Oh happy the mole
> With tunnels to spare
> he loves to catch wormies
> he loves to catch wormies
> and eat dry worm pie
> with a slug, slug, slug, slug
> and a truffle or two
> I'll lay my traps
> and hail the new moon
> with a slug, slug, slug, slug
> and a truffle or two
> I'll lay my traps
> and hail the new moon.

Ben stopped in his tracks by the white gate. He peered below the lowest bar. "Bless my soul alive," he breathed, "the garden of many fragrances . . . it's gone." I stared blankly at the big ploughed field which came nearly to the edge of the barn. The grey furrows played with a grey sky so it was hard to say where the horizon started.

"Gone," he repeated before hurrying under the bar.

I followed closely behind him, keeping to a narrow strip of turf by the barn overrun with pineapple weed and last year's ratstail.

"It was here," said Ben pausing by the far corner of the barn, pointing to the edge of the field. He did not stop but hurried round the corner.

I found him, lying flat on his face where he had tripped over a root. He picked himself up and waved an angry claw at the root.

"I nearly broke my neck then. Just take more care in future." He kicked the root once and kicked it again, then hurried to the five-bar gate which led into the inner quadrangle.

The farm buildings had once been a glory, but that was in another time. The large, rough chalk blocks were still there as well as the red brick which ran as high as the old elder trees. Many of the peg tiles had skidded off in the high winds, and those which hadn't were held in place by large saucers of green moss and thick yellow strands of lichen. The rain had cracked the mortar between the blocks of chalk and flint and brick, and, where the lintels had collapsed, the roof was held up by the ivy which crept up the posts and where the lintels had been. A row of great beeches towered over the buildings, leaning slightly, blown that way by the winds which came over the Downs. It was quiet inside the courtyard, not that there was any wind, but the walls and the ground which had once been laid with flint, were covered with old growth. Along the inner walls the tangle of weeds still raged, the nettles beating the docks and cow parsley; in the damper corners I saw the shine of silverweed, and woolly thistles starred the ground in front of us. It was silent in the courtyard, a burial mound of a sort. Not the brave dead mounds of Lambourn, at least they have their visitors. No-one came here except master moles and their apprentices.

"Isn't it wonderful," said Ben sightwhiskering every corner. "To think no-one ever comes here. What peace. What isolation. No clients. No thinking. Wonderful," he sighed.

"Wouldn't you get lonely?" I asked.

"Impossible to get lonely. That's just the trouble. I wish I could." He turned over a brick. He looked furtively from side to side. He whispered to me: "The crawlies . . . they're too nosy, always poking their feelers into my business. You can never get away from them. It's a curse."

He pointed to a drain between two woolly thistles. "That, by the way, is where we are going. It is the home of the Badger of the Four Ways, or Burley Pickles to his friends."

I peered into the drain expecting something poohy, but instead an agreeable sweet smell wafted upwards. Ben smelt it too.

"Ah. My favourite!"

He heaved against a thistle.

I thought he had cracked in half.

To my astonishment the thistle moved. He pushed harder.

"All right, all right," said a deep savoury voice from down the drain. "I can hear you. I'm coming."

There was a loud rustle somewhere underground. A pair of large claws gripped the edges of the drain. A striped face appeared out of the gloom.

"Blow me tight," said the deep savoury voice. "If it isn't Ben of Thornshade. Welcome."

Chapter Seven

Burley Pickles was the most agreeable badger I have ever met, not that I have met many, for they are notoriously shy and next to moles difficult to approach unless by appointment. It says a lot for the calm and assurance of his mind that at no time did he express surprise at my presence but acknowledged me with a nod of his wizened head. He was a creature of the most refined manners, the nearest thing to a gentleman I ever met in the hedgerows. But I don't want to mislead you. He was also very fussy and particular, lazy and with terrible table manners.

Though the business which brought us at such short notice must have been important, he made us feel at home after our journey, not pressing us with questions until we had rested and eaten the spread he had prepared. Unlike Ben's bleak office, I found myself in comfortable surroundings with mounds of leaves for chairs, and with bark strips around the walls to keep the damp and roots out. I had the feeling I was in a private study rather than a hole. Everything looked so spacious, and as for light, there were none of the gloomy shadows and flickerings of Thornshade. It was obvious a lot of thought had gone into the business of lighting. I saw the same rock crystals, but instead of being piled on top of each other, they had been tastefully dotted round the walls and all over the ceiling. In fact, there was so much light, I thought I was looking at the Milky Way. I could see the flints and traces of mortar in the roof, and there were several wooden pillars, the bottoms of the posts which supported the building. The air circulated gently, probably from some special ventilation shafts, and there was no hard, itchy straw but a thick layer of leaves which kept you warm and comfortable at the same time.

Pickles had flopped on a large pile of leaves. He was leaning back on one elbow and eyeing hungrily a round flat stone covered with all manner of strange things. He invited us to join him. We sat by the stone and looked at the spread before us. There were beech nuts, hazel nuts and dried chestnuts; there was dry worm pie, beetles on sticks, smoked slugs, pickled grasshoppers, and for afters there was a selection of crab apples, truffles and birch sap pudding.

"After you," said Pickles graciously.

"No, after you," I said stupidly.

I could not believe my eyes. Pickles lunged forward grabbing half the food into his corner. He scraped it into a pile so the chestnuts were mixed with the smoked slugs, the truffles with the beetles on sticks. He did not bother to lift it into his mouth, but, barely pausing for breath, he gobbled the food direct from the table sending bits flying everywhere. The food rapidly disappeared, but not until Ben had grabbed his share and matched his friend's own excesses. I was forced to snatch at things otherwise I would have gone hungry.

"Nothing like dinner," squeaked Ben contentedly, as he flopped back onto the leaves.

"Just what I say," agreed Pickles who continued licking his claws clean.

I was disgusted but said nothing. I sat down on the leaves looking at the table and the surrounding floor which was covered with scraps of food.

"Shouldn't we clean up?" I suggested.

"Clean up?" said Pickles, "Of course." he snapped his claws on the stone.

I heard a rustling somewhere behind me and fast skipping sounds. From the corners and behind pillars, running and hopping, came four dark shapes with long scaly tails. Two of the rats flew onto the stone, the other two dived and fought between themselves for the remaining scraps. They cleared every crumb before disappearing back into the corners and behind the pillars.

Ben coughed to clear his throat. It was the time for introductions. He rubbed his claws together and peered into the starry sky as if for inspiration, but it looked to me like a grand pose.

"The search is over, Pickles. At last I have found someone to replace Flit The Wren. He has done the basic training and I think has the makings of a detective in our line of business. He is weak-minded, lazy, disobedient, easily bored, given to imagining things. In short, let me introduce you. Burley Pickles—Fellman Clack."

"My pleasure," said Pickles warmly without getting up from the floor.

I smiled weakly and sat down again. I was thinking of the rats.

Ben sat down. Pickles sat up. It was his turn for introductions.

He had a mellow, deep voice as if the words had to bubble up from a great depth. He spoke easily and warmly from a never ending supply of breath.

"There's not much to say really," he said, keeping down a yawn. "I live at the Four Ways, do the odd job or two, and generally take things very easy."

"You're too modest," said Ben ticking off his friend with a waving claw.

Pickles grinned and I could hardly conceal my fascination as I watched the furfolds crease generously across his face. "Yes. I like to take things easy. Why hurry? The trees don't. Huhuhuhuh."

There was a long silence as Pickles paused in his thinking. His head rocked contentedly on his broad shoulders and though he faced Ben and me from across the table, he stared past us lost in some pleasant reverie.

I was thinking too much of the rats. I was getting impatient. Ben restrained me with a sharp glance.

Something was happening to Pickles. His eyebrows shot up at the ends to meet in a deep trough at the middle. His white-tipped ears trembled along with his stumpy tail which swished among the leaves. The rest of his body was rigid. He jumped from the leaves as he spoke.

"*Of course*," his voice exploded, "you want to know why you came here." He looked at Ben, then me. "Tonight there will be another visitor . . . the White Rook."

Ben whistled with surprise.

"Yes, he will be with us soon and I hear he is in a very bad mood. It's come right in the middle of nesting and you know how he hates to travel when he is busy." He added as an afterthought: "I wonder what it can all be about?"

Ben rubbed his whiskers thoughtfully but said nothing.

Pickles continued: "I suggest we have a nice little nap. You must be tired after your journey and you never know when the White Rook will appear."

Pickles set the example by half-burying himself in a mound of leaves. Ben quickly followed, and by the time I had stretched out I could hear the steady snoring of my two companions. I went to sleep.

* * * * *

In my sleep, otherwise black and empty, I saw a strange thing. I was on top of a hill or had the eyes of a bird, for I could see a great distance. There was a skyline every way I turned. I could not recognise the land for there was no green or living thing that I could see. It was grey and jagged, and instead of trees there were flames leaping from the ground and black boulders of every size. I was with other children on the hill. We were holding hands and holding the hands of a lady with long hair and she was dressed in green. We were looking for something in the distance. One of the children pointed to something on the horizon. We all looked that way. There was something coming. It was a long way off. It was white on the skyline and it was travelling at great speed. We watched holding hands, keeping close to the green lady.

I woke roughly from this sleep. A claw was shaking me from side to side. I looked into something blurred and stripy. It was Pickles and he was whispering.

"The White Rook has arrived."

I sat up quickly and looked round the room. There was no sign of the White Rook. Ben was by the stone, Pickles by my side.

"I can't see him," I said irritably.

"*Haven't you got eyebrains?*" cackled someone behind me.

I sprang up and dived into the leaves for cover.

The laughter continued, swelled by the squeaking and bellowing of my two companions.

"Call yourself a detective," I heard the White Rook say. "He'll want to sleep in lavender next." The laughter continued.

I stood and wiped the leaves from my face. I wish I hadn't for I was not prepared for the size and appearance of the Rook. He was bigger than any crow, and though not pure white, white enough to earn himself the title. He was a freak among thousands, a formidable Rook, with deeply set black eyes rolling on either side of an enormous shovel of a beak.

He flapped his wings so the leaves flew across the room.

"So, this is the new apprentice is it?" He did not move nearer but stretched out his neck, so the feathers ruffling his throat stood out one by one.

"The White Rook—Fellman Clack," said Ben getting the introductions over.

The dark eyes examined me from toes to curly hair. They swivelled on Ben. His head returned to normal, half sunk between his feather-plated wings.

"I'm happy to meet you, Fellman," he said more gently, rocking from one claw to another. Then his wings shot into the air and his tail feathers banged the floor. "*But I'm not happy do you hear?*" he squawked to the others.

His broad beak followed his eyes as they darted on both sides, suspecting every shadow. He flapped onto the round stone and peered among the night lights above our heads. There was a rustle in the corner.

"What's that?" he squawked.

"The rats I think," said Pickles.

"Get them out."

Pickles ordered them to leave by the side tunnels.

The White Rook was in a foul mood, there was no doubt about that. I knew from Ben that he lived at the far end of Blowingstone Wood, but not in a large rookery for he had been driven away because of his colour. He lived by himself, more like a crow. I could not work out his association with Ben or Pickles but whatever it was, he was regarded with a certain reverence, even fear.

He spoke as the willow burns, with great spits, cracklings, hissings, and gaps which count as silences. He either perched on the stone or strutted round it, rubbing his wings together as if he were trying to keep warm. He stretched his neck and cawed to clear his throat.

"Yeeeeeees yeeees," he hissed slowly, fanning his tail feathers and arching his back so he looked twice as big. He had the uncanny habit of being able to swivel his eyes in opposite directions, so as he spoke one eye rested on my two companions, the other on me.

"Yeeees," he hissed again, "problems, problems, problems. What a business it all is. Where do they come from?"

He looked at us. We looked blankly at each other.

"Yes where do they come from? And just when I was settling down to nesting." He strutted round the table, his head and beak sinking lower and lower until it almost scraped the stone.

"Yeees everyone wants me to make them happy. I tell you it's a wretched life. *A wretched life do you hear*!" His voice softened. "Whatever happened to the good old days, when you could just open you beak and in would fly roast earwig pie? Instead, what is there? Problems, problems, problems. There's nothing to eat. I'm getting thin. Look."

He raised one wing above his head. "See? Nothing but feathers and bone. I'll be a scarecrow soon."

He marched round the stone a little faster. "Problems, problems, problems. Everyone is trying to solve problems. And do you think there are any less?" He swivelled his eyes upon us.

We looked blankly at each other.

"I'll tell you. *No. No. No.* There are even more."

His tail feathers flapped on the stone louder and louder. He chooked twice to clear his throat. "I once knew a creature, a noisy, quarrelsome, petty-minded, fidgeting shadow tail of a squirrel, one of those poor creatures that hunt for roses on thistle heads. Every day this squirrel counted his berries to make sure none were stolen. He came to me in a state. He said he could never sleep. I told him his head was full of figures and I would be crazy if I knew so much. He said: 'You must be mad. I'm educating myself. I can count more than anybody else. What's wrong with that? Are you against education?' 'Fine,' I told him, 'but where does it all lead?' 'Simple,' he said, 'the more I count the more I learn, and the more I learn the more I find and the more I find the more there is to solve, and so the more there is to solve the less I know, and the less I know the more help I need and that's why I am going crazy.'

"Hahahahahahahahah," squawked the White Rook, flapping his wings hard against his sides. "He was crazy too mark my words. Hahahahahahah."

He sighed. "Yeeees it's not so simple living. They're out to get you all right."

He turned sharply to face Pickles. "Remember the song, the one we sang to frighten that mad fox?"

"Of course," boomed Pickles cheerfully.

"Yees, we have got to know what we are up against."

The White Rook crouched, arching his wings above him like white sails. He swayed from side to side, stamping one claw then another, shuffling in small circles and nearly scraping his beak against the stone. He sang in a broken crackling voice.

We are the shadows of the night
out to give you a fright
in the darkest twiiiiilight
in the paaaaaaaalest moonlight
We'll be waiting.

Don't venture far at night
to terrify you is our delight
when you're thinking we're not here
like some ghastly dream which reappears
We'll be waiting.

He spun round on his claws, cackling nastily under his breath, and beating his wings so the air fanned in our faces.

We're out to get you tonight
Paranoia is our delight
where the ivy clings to the trees
and branches crack like a dead crow's wheeze
we'll be waiting.
Hahahahahahahahahaha
Ohohohohohohohohohohoho
We're out to get you tonight.

His horrible laughter faded.
"More more," shouted both Pickles and Ben.
"Do you know what's out there? Have you seen them?"
He swivelled his eyes on Pickles and me.
"Do you know what we are up against?"
There was a long pause. "We saw them from the crossroads," said Ben. "They were as dark as a centipede in a hole. They were as dark as a night sky, but it was the daytime . . . I don't know what they were."
"Nor does anybody else," snapped the White Rook. "And that's not all." He stretched out his neck and whispered ominously. "Have you noticed the flowers are late. Where are the humbees, the nettle-scrapers, the little things you can't see, the green growing shoots, the things that crawl in the night, the day songs, the night songs and the buds on my beloved elms? *Where are they!*"
He strutted backwards and forwards, sideways and round-

ways, crossways and lengthways. He stopped. "It just isn't natural. And now this."

Pickles broke the silence with the questions we all wanted to ask. "Why have you called us here? What can we do?"

"There is nothing we can do but we must do something. That is why I called you here. We are all detectives and fitted to the task. We have to find out what is happening, and though my nest might get broken while I am away, better a broken nest than a broken heart. Are you with me?"

There was no hesitation. "Yes," we all cried.

Chapter Eight

Pickles was reluctant to get up next morning. "I think," he said, yawning, "I would be much more useful in bed." There was silence. "Besides, I haven't thought of one good reason to get up yet." He wriggled to bury himself deeper in the leaves. "And besides again," we heard his muffled voice, "I think I've got a bit of a cold." As if to prove his point a handful of leaves flew into the air as he sneezed.

Ben and I were squatting by the table. The White Rook was perched on the edge. We were having breakfast.

"These are delicious worms," squeaked Ben as he stuffed another clawful into his mouth.

"Mmmmmm, and these nuts," cawed the White Rook, "lovely." He winked at us. "What are you doing Ben, there'll be none left for anybody else."

The bed of leaves burst open and a hot lumbering creature joined us at the table. "I've been thinking it over," said Pickles. "What's a little cold anyway?"

Excitement was in the air at breakfast, not that the food lasted long when Pickles arrived. My own mind sparked like an open fire, and I could see that behind a cool exterior even Ben could not stop his tail swishing and thumping the leaves. So now we were four I thought. I was growing to like the White Rook but I was put off by his swashbuckling manner, his breeziness and the way he had of making you feel smaller than a fly in a cowpie. He had lightning changes of character, one moment a clown with a voice as soft as thistledown, the next he would be hard and cutting as thistle spikes, expecting you to snap when he snapped, jump when he jumped.

He was impatient, cunning, subtle, gross, larger than life. Fearless in a word. He had a way of making us believe in him, want to follow him. He was our leader. He was our fool, and he would die laughing if he had to.

There were no crumbs to clear as Pickles licked the table clean. When he had finished the White Rook strutted round the table, occasionally jabbing his beak at an imaginary prey.

"That's what I'd do." He jabbed the empty air. "Try to frighten me would they?" He jabbed and jabbed again. He looked at us, rolling his eyes either side of his broad beak.

"Yeeees we have to do something . . . before it is too late. My messengers are out watching and reporting. They see what others dare not see. They go where others have not been. They bring a strange story. They have seen them with their own eyes."

He pointed with his wings. "They have seen them here and there and everywhere. Nowhere is safe. When owlight comes they return to the hills beyond the White Horse."

"That far?" whistled Ben.

"Yeees that far. Even my eyes, bless their souls alive, do not venture that far." He searched our faces, swivelling one eye on Pickles, the other on Ben and me. "No-one dares to go there. I am told there is not a living sound a mile around the White Horse except, except," his voice got softer and softer, "for the sound they make."

"What sound?" whispered Pickles, twisting uncomfortably in the leaves.

"A sound so horrible, it would scare a lich-owl. Hahahahahahah." He flapped his wings and stamped his claws.

"I don't think that was funny," said Pickles. He had dived into the leaves and was just surfacing.

There was silence except for the steady tread of the White Rook's claws on the stone.

"What I don't understand," said Pickles, now sitting sensibly by the stone, "it sounds like a lot of starlings to me. What's wrong with starlings? They always fly together in hard winters but they'll split up soon when they get the nest fever. What's all the fuss?''

The White Rook threw up his wings in despair. ''You short-sighted son of a horseshoe bat. Do you think I don't know that?''

He turned to Ben for support but the master detective appeared to be dozing by the side of the stone.

''No,'' cawed the White Rook ruffling his coarse wing feathers and shaking his beak as if ticking off a naughty child. ''They are starlings all right . . . and something else too, something which hasn't got a name. My eyes have sent many reports. They all see the starlings, and it is a terrible sight to see so many, but they see something else too, and none of them can agree what it is.''

''What is it?''

''One swears he saw an eagle flying with them.''

''An eagle?'' interrupted Pickles with surprise, wriggling his white-tipped ears. ''But there aren't any eagles here.''

''Exactly. There are no eagles here. Another saw a band of wild dogs, with horrible faces and bones sticking out from their sides. Another heard the cry of hungry hoverhawks, another saw the hollow eyes of men with shooting sticks. Shall I go on?''

''No, no no,'' said Pickles whose fur now quivered on end, ''that's enough thank you.''

Ben was still slumped over the side of the stone.

The White Rook clapped his wings above his furry head.

Ben stirred, scratching his head. He turned towards me. He sightwhiskered me carefully, taking deep sniffs as he did so. There were puzzled furfolds across his face.

''What is it?'' I asked.

The others looked at us. I got embarrassed.

Ben grabbed the edge of the stone and stood on his hindclaws.

''It's a strange thing,'' he said slowly, ''but when I notthink on all this I keep seeing you and something in your hand. A shining thing.''

''What?''

''A shining thing with something old on it. A carving.''

I searched my pockets. I remembered that I had put the

ivory square in my pouch. I undid the strap. The others gathered around me to see what was there. I pulled out the box of matches with one match, two pieces of liquorice toffee I was keeping for a special occasion, my penknife, and last of all, the carving. I put it on the table.

"Is this what you mean?" I pushed it towards Ben.

Ben wedged it between his claws and held it against his tiny eyes. He tapped it with his claws, licked it, then rubbed it against his snout to pick out the design edges.

I could not understand what was happening, nor could the others. Ben fanned his whiskers excitedly and wobbled on his claws. He gripped the stone with both foreclaws. He spoke, but not in his quickfire way, nor did he speak to any of us in particular, but the words sprang from him like water, bubbling from his depths and full of feeling.

"It's true. It's true. After all this time. It's true. I never believed it was true. I can't believe it. It's true. It's true."

"What's true?" squawked the White Rook. "Tell us."

Ben raised the carving in his claw. He held it so we could see it clearly. "This is the sign of Wormhole the First, my great-great-great-great-great-grandmole, the founder of our detective business. The first in the great line of mole detectives."

"How do you know?" asked the White Rook not bothering to conceal his doubts.

"There is a story in our family that Wormhole died on a long journey, a journey from which he never recovered, a journey which led to the sound of the star breaking."

Both Pickles and the White Rook winced at the mention of the star breaking.

"At the end of his life, so the story goes, his mind cracked, he wandered off smilecreasing into the hills. He left without warning and without leaving a message."

Ben pointed to one side of the ivory. "That divided circle inside a square is the sign of our line of moles."

"It's the one outside your office," I said, remembering the carved wooden sign.

"That's right. It is the sign of the master detective. I use it to recognise myself."

"Let me see," said the White Rook ignoring the last

arrogant remark. "Yeees it is very old, and so worn. But what's all this on the other side? It looks like a cat's walk to me. I can't make head or tail of it."

We looked at both sides of the square, and this, drawn about four times larger, is what we saw:

"It's got to mean something," squeaked Ben, hardly able to contain his excitement.

Pickles squinted at it through half-closed eyes.

I found the lines a meaningless jumble, a cat's walk as the White Rook had said. They could have meant anything. The more we looked the more frustrated grew Ben.

"It must mean something," he squeaked even louder.

"Of course," boomed Pickles who had stepped back two paces from the table. "You're too near to see it. I know what it is now." He pointed to the right-hand corner. "Now run your eyes through the middle. Imagine those curvy lines are legs, and what have you got?"

The White Rook cackled in agreement. "Yeees, of course. Clever old Pickles. I can see it now. It's the White Horse and its funny beak."

We looked at it again but no-one could decipher the other scratchings.

"It looks like a maze to me," said Pickles after looking from several different angles. "I can't understand it. They look like nibbled pine cones, or a mushroom, or tunnels. It could be anything.''

All this deeply affected Ben. He squatted for he was getting unsteady on his claws. He scratched his whiskers nervously, and the intensity of his silence silenced us.

"Bit your tongue?" said the White Rook playfully, swivelling an eye on Pickles and winking at me.

Ben turned to me. He spoke with considerable effort. "Where did you find it? It's important."

I told him the little I knew, how my mother had found it in my pocket though I had no idea how it had got there. Despite Ben's questions there was nothing I could add. All this had a bad effect on Ben who had the air of someone trembling with secret thoughts. The unseen strain creased the furfolds across his face.

He rose from the floor and thrust his claws behind his back. He shuffled slowly round the table, stopping every so often to keep his balance.

"There is something I have never told you about Wormhole, something you ought to know. You won't find it in any stories, for it has been a secret in our family. As you know, Wormhole was a popular figure and had many clients. There is good reason to think that he was excited by the travel stories he heard. Though he never travelled much he collected souvenirs from far away places, and it is known that he often accepted something glittering, such as a peacock feather, in exchange for his services. He died young and in strange circumstances. The stories say he died with a smilecrease. It is only half the truth.

"The stories say he went off into the hills. This is true, but there is something else. Before he died, he told his apprentice Mowdiworp he was on the greatest case of his lifetime, the puzzle to outpuzzle the rest. There are only a few facts we are sure of, and one is that his client was a bat, and the case was so fascinating that Wormhole did something he had never done before. He put Mowdiworp in charge and left Thornshade to make a journey. Where he went we do not know, though it was somewhere west. The story goes that he was never seen again.''

He paused.

"It isn't true.''

Pickles and the White Rook gasped.

"His apprentice found his body at the top of Thornshade. He had died within whistling distance of home. He did not die with a smile on his whiskers. He died of fright. It's true. As if he had seen his worst fear. By his body was a small bone carving showing his findings. As you know it used to be our custom to carve solutions to cases on bone or anything hard. Wormhole was buried with his carving somewhere near Thornshade. Neither has been seen since. All we know is that on one side was a square divided by a circle, which was adopted thereafter as the sign of the business."

Ben clawed the ivory square.

"I believe this to be the very same carving. If we could understand it . . . we would have the solution of Wormhole's last case."

We looked at each other with unconcealed astonishment.

"At the time," continued Ben, "it was considered bad for business to tell the truth, so his body was buried secretly. The stories sprang up of course, but the truth was never known. There were no marks on his body. We know he journeyed a great distance for his claws were worn to the bone. Where he went, what he saw, what the case was about, no-one knows. They have remained questions passed down the generations from Mowdiworp and finally to me. I often think about them and what would make him break the habits of a lifetime. There must have been something precious at the end of the journey."

"Like the buried treasure of the fairy tales," added Pickles, "between Wayland's Smithy and Uffington Castle."

"Yes, there are such stories and Wormhole would have known them too. But he was no bluebottle on stilts, something must have convinced him that a long journey would have its rewards."

"This is all very interesting," said the White Rook, "but what has it got to do with our journey to find where the starlings roost?"

Ben scratched his fur one way and then the other. "Nothing, I think," he said slowly, "but I have the strangest feeling that I'll find out on the way.''

* * * * *

We dropped the matter after that, taking the White Rook's counsel that much had to be planned, a route chosen and food found enough for the journey.

It was decided that three of Pickles' rats should accompany us, to act as bearers, tunnellers, and, in case of emergencies, a larger number would be safer. The White Rook objected at first, saying there would not be enough food, but changed his mind when he saw it would save time foraging. I made three bags, one for each of the rats, using some scraps of sackcloth I found in one of the barns. Pickles fussed like a hen with one chick, gathering nuts, dried worms, bark strips, grains, snails and other provisions, while Ben and the White Rook stayed in a corner discussing the merits of different routes. Occasionally their voices bubbled over in disagreement.

For myself I was light-headed with excitement. My mind fizzed with a hundred thoughts. I longed to return to the outside world, for that is how I saw it now, to travel under the blue sky and among familiar places. I had lived too long from the green trees and grass beneath my feet. I was homesick but I did not know it.

The White Rook, used to the pecking order of rooks, quickly took control before our departure. While Pickles and I squatted by the table filling the food bags, he paraded

in front of the rats, fanning his tail feathers and stiffly arching his back. He strutted with short, determined steps, and gave what would pass in military circles as a pep talk.

"Riiiight. You have all volunteered to help in a most important mission."

"What is it?" asked one of the rats.

"We are going where none have been before, to find the starling roost on the hills beyond White Horse Hill."

"Is it far?" asked the same rat.

"I'll ask the questions," said the White Rook swivelling his eyes on him. "You know what happened to the wide-mouthed toad, don't you?"

"No" said the rat.

"It's just as well," said the White Rook, "for if you did you wouldn't ask so many questions."

There was a long silence.

"Excuse me, " said a small squeaking voice. "What happened to the wide-mouthed toad?"

"He asked one too many questions and fell into a fox's mouth." He peered into the eyes of the rat. "Be sure you don't follow him."

There were no more questions. We were ready to leave.

Chapter Nine

I do not believe I had ever seen such a morning as the one that day. We left by another route into the courtyard and the first thing we saw was a chalk blue sky and the light sparkling on the branches of the beeches. When we reached grass level we arrived on the shore of a white sea. A blanket of drifting mist covered the courtyard, spreading far beyond the gate and into the ploughed field. It was thick enough to shroud the ground, and through it poked the stems of cow parsley, nettles and thistles. There had been a heavy frost too. The light danced on the redbrick walls, and, in the corners, there were circular glistening patterns where the spiders had been busy.

I could hardly see the White Rook in the mist, except when he flew to perch on the ivy twining round the post above our heads.

He flapped his wings together for warmth. "Blow me tight," he said hunching deeper into his feathers, "if you ever wished you was a swallow now's the time to wish it." His frantic efforts to stay warm knocked a shower of ice crystals to the ground.

"It's all very well," grumbled Pickles tiptoeing over a puddle of ice, "but wouldn't it be better if we postponed it; had a nap or something?"

"Postponed it? It's perfect," said the White Rook. "Even bluebottles will stay at home. You have to be mad to go out in this weather."

"He's right," said Ben.

"Of course I'm right," snapped the White Rook.

There was no turning back. Pickles reluctantly led our party through the tumbling arch of ivy and into the courtyard. I would have called it a silent world had it not been for Ben's lessons on the art of listening. The sounds were everywhere; it was a case of hearing one to hear the others. The frost held everything in its hoary fingers, and the silver-lined grasses on the path tinkled with jingle jangle edges as we brushed past them. The mist muffled the footfalls, as well as the breathing. Everywhere were sliding sounds, thawing sounds, dripping sounds and the steady pad of Pickles trotting up front. A master of little hard-to-see sounds and scents, and with an unswerving sense of direction, he led us through his home territory as if feeling his way in the dark, stopping to sightwhisker when he was unsure but never getting flustered when we strayed from the path. Not that we strayed far from the path, for he was taking us along a run he had known all his life, one that led to the Four Ways and the Ridgeway which we were to follow. We skirted the farm buildings sticking to the wild flower path. We travelled slowly but it was fast enough that morning.

After the five-bar gate the White Rook ordered us to keep a strict single file. He walked alongside us, usually silent but sometimes talking with Ben about the route, or dropping back to encourage the bearers. Occasionally he flew onto a thorn bush to get a clearer view. We kept to the side of the track, between the grass verge and the first of the three ruts. The mist was thicker here than in the courtyard but it was still possible to see Ben when he stood on his hind claws.

I gave up crawling at this stage, having discovered, if painfully, that it was easier to walk on two legs. I was not prepared for the muscle cramps in my back or the effect it would have on my companions. Only a sharp command from the White Rook stopped the rats from fleeing into the hedgerow, and, for a moment, even Ben twittered in the way he does when something surprises him. Pickles, with his plodding nature, took it in his stride and his calm helped calm things down. After that the rats insisted they travelled up front alongside Pickles, with Ben and the White Rook between them and myself.

The White Rook was already at the Four Ways when we arrived, having flown on ahead. He was perched on top of a white signpost, pointing to the Ridgeway east and west, Lambourn to the south and Kingston Lisle to the north. It was hard to know we were on top of the world for there was no breeze or view. On either side as far as we could see ancient hedgerows skirted the trackway. A river of mist flowed between them, with points of light dancing, disappearing, as the early sun caught the tall frozen grasses. Above it all, and at the end of the view, was the shining blue sky.

We followed Pickles into the long grass by the side of the hedge. I still remember those moments of silence as we rested on an island of grass hummocks above the level of the mist, waiting for the word to leave. We felt keenly, more so as it was unspoken, that once on the Ridgeway there could be no turning back. The Four Ways was safe harbour and we could still see the farm buildings and the towering shadows of the beeches drawn against the sky. If we looked the other way, only the ever-changing mist and the dark walls of the hedgerows marked our course. It led to uncharted areas, and even the White Rook, who had flown over most of the Vale, had never ventured into the downs. As for the Ridgeway, it was a well-known passageway for young foxes and a favourite hunting ground for hoverhawks. Our path lay due west along its winding course to the White Horse ramparts, known as Uffington Castle, and beyond that into the distant hills.

I said we all rested, but Ben, tireless worker that he was, preferred to scout a few yards up the track. He vanished in the mist but I heard him crawling in his clumsy breast-stroke, scratching the ground with his claws and stopping occasionally to have a good sniff. He popped through the mist about ten yards away, on the far side of the track. He sightwhiskered to find us and then dived back under. He was crawling by the hedgerow.

The White Rook flew down and I watched him land with his wings outstretched. He disappeared in the mist, and we heard him strutting over the hard grass edges. The first thing we saw were the blacks of his eyes. It frightened us all until we saw his wings emerge from the mist. He pulled himself onto the grass platform.

"Yeeees. Perfect, perfect. Not a sign of life anywhere. Have we all rested?"

I looked at the plump white and black markings by my side.

"I suppose so," muttered Pickles not moving. "That's just the trouble," he said sniffing and showing more signs of life, "the smell. There's a funny smell here."

"Smell? I can't smell anything," said the White Rook blowing and sucking air through the holes at the top of his beak.

"Just what I mean. There isn't any smell. No tracks, no clues, no sign of anything. In fact, I don't think anything has been this way for a long time."

The White Rook had no time to answer. Somewhere from the mist came a high pitched voice.

"Don't move."

The dark, pointed snout of Ben surfaced in the middle of the track, opposite us.

"Stay where you are."

I could see he was carefully fanning his whiskers at something we could not see. He was going round in ever decreasing circles, dipping below the mist to surface a yard nearer, then vanishing to reappear again even closer. I could see he was working with the speed of a ferret, peering and snorting into every crack. He stopped only once, and that was a pause to wipe the frost from his whiskers before continuing with his detective work. When he reached our side he sped back under the mist and popped up in the centre of the track. He undid the strap of his pouch and there was a sound of something being scraped onto a piece of bark. There was a quick shuffling noise and he appeared beside

Pickles, giving him a start.

We watched without a word as he undid his pouch. He placed the find in front of us. We sniffed it in turn. I felt it with my fingers. It was about the size of a blackcurrant, except it was spongey with hard bits, like shells, in it. It was brown and had a fusty smell.

"Do you know what this is?" asked Ben.

We all knew it was a dropping but no-one knew what it was. Pickles thought it was a hedge vole, but the rats said it was too big. They thought it was a squirrel. The White Rook could not make up his mind. I said nothing.

After a long pause, waiting for the last of the speculation and guesses, Ben took the centre of the circle and shuffled round it clockwise, with his claws thrust behind his back and a distant look on his whiskers.

"Unless I am mistaken, and that is very unlikely, this is no ordinary dropping." He sniffed it again. "I have made a little study of this subject, and judging from what I think is a mixture of hairy dung beetles, and chrysalis cockchafers, I have little doubt that it belongs to a bat."

"A bat?" we all said.

"Yes a bat. A greater horseshoe bat to be specific."

"Hang on," said Pickles trying to be reasonable, "aren't they extinct in this area?"

"Exactly. A nice point." He paused. "And another thing. This is not an extinct dropping. It is fresh this morning."

"Do you really have to frighten the rats," said the White Rook trying to coax them back from the depths of the hedge.

"Who's afraid of a little bat anyway?" He flapped his wings, rolled his eyes, stretched his neck full length and jabbed the empty air. "See. It's easy. Besides," he added, "they don't fly by day."

It had the desired effect. The rats took up their position alongside Pickles. I followed behind Ben and the White Rook behind me. We left our little grass island to sink slowly, step by step, into the mist flowing and glinting its way to the west.

* * * * *

I can hardly describe the blueness of the sky that day, let alone the feelings I kept to myself. Since standing I had felt different, a different shape. I had one foot in the world of names—moles, trees, butterflies and boys—but I wasn't sure what my name was. My other half belonged to Ben's world which is as nameless as the wind in the trees, where shapes all depend on the way you look at them. I had always thought of trees as being heavy solid things that didn't move, but for Ben they were light and free, and certainly did not always stay in one place. You must understand that Ben had never seen a tree. He was too short-sighted. He felt trees. He saw them from the inside where there are no names, only faces, changing with the way you see them. They were his companions, the way he was my companion. If sometimes I found his world strange it was because we looked closely at things, in the same way a familiar face is strange when seen unexpectedly. That day I felt I was walking between two worlds and belonged to neither. I had nothing to call my own.

The day was fast brightening. I could tell for the sun was higher than the walls of the hedges, and the frost was steaming on the dark criss-crossed branches. We kept to the centre of the track, where the mist flowed deepest, and sometimes the whole party vanished and the white river came as high as my jumper. It was like that all along the crest until Ram's Hill where the hedgerow stopped on the bald slopes. The mist flowed down the sides, and it wasn't until we found a high patch in the long grass that we could see the White Horse Vale. The low-lying hills were its distant shores, and where the white waves ran along the blue sky, I recognised one or two woods breaking darkly on the horizon. There was nothing else. I looked onto a white world and I felt a stranger.

We stayed in the long grass eating some of the food carried by the rats, keeping silent for there were no words to describe the emptiness of that view. Pickles became the eyes for Ben, who could only sightwhisker great spaces, and the voice for all those feelings we kept to ourselves. He did not speak but sang in a slow deep voice as we lay hidden in the grass looking into the Vale. His notes rang clearly in the

Downland air.

> O Corn spirit maybe sometime
> I'll find those waters
> Leading to your shrine
> And there by the dark oak tree
> down by the bubbling spring
> I'll sit and I'll deeply breathe
> This song of thanksgiving
> O corn spirit maybe sometime
> O corn spirit maybe sometime
> O corn spirit maybe sometime
> O corn spirit maybe sometime

The silence lasted long after the notes had faded. None of us could bring ourselves to move. Even the White Rook was unusually quiet, turning his back to us to search the sky. I could see his tail feathers were trembling with concealed feelings. Ben sighed and twittered. The rats stayed silent. The song had us in its spell. Pickles settled further into the grass, resting his muzzle on his claw, watching the mist tumble down the slopes, past the frozen fields and murky lines of hedgerows. There was not a breath of wind, not a squeak or a small thump.

Ben stood and shuffled across to Pickles, whispering something into his ear. They looked at us, and there was the smallest smilecrease on Ben's whiskers. The White Rook quizzed them with his quizzing eyes.

Pickles, who always crawled everywhere, jerked himself upright, steadying himself by placing one claw on top of Ben's head. Ben was standing, mimicking Pickles' lurching movements from side to side. They both kept straight faces.

Pickles snorted to clear his throat and Ben squeaked to clear his. They were swaying together now. There were glugging, rumbling noises from Pickles as if a barrel of oil was being emptied. Ben whistled through his teeth; Pickles did the same but an octave lower. They copied each other, leaning forward towards us, beckoning us with one foreclaw. The rats sniggered. The White Rook guffawed, clapping his wings above his back. It was Pickles' fairy song.

It's not in the morning that I sing this song
It's not in the evening when shadows grow long
It's not in the twilight, at dusk or at dawn,
but when I'm asleep and I'm about to yaaaaaawwn

Then I remember the time on my rounds one moon day
I came to the stump where I often did play
I rubbed and I rubbed and when I was done
A strange little voice by my side now began.

(His deep voice trailed away, and Ben's high piping voice
sang:)

wusha nini di-di wusha nina di-di
wusha nina di-di wusha nina di-di
wusha nina di-di wusha nina di-di
wusha na nina di-di

I stared at the leaves and a sight I did see
I saw a strange thing with two eyes and one wing
It had bogey arms and it had a green tail
It flew to the stump and continued to wail

wusha nini di-di wusha nina di-di
wusha nina di-di wusha nina di-di
wusha nina di-di wusha nina di-di
wusha na nina di-di

I jumped up at once and I bowed to the ground
I thought I would make a melodious sound
I started to sing but a frog caught my throat
Instead of the music came only these notes

wusha nini di-di wusha nina di-di
wusha nina di-di wusha nina di-di
wusha nina di-di wusha nina di-di
wusha na nina di-di

The two danced to a standstill and fell on all fours.
We collapsed in laughter but no-one laughed louder than
the White Rook who laughed longest. He swayed backwards
and forwards, laughing with his beak open so you could see
his tongue waggling inside.

"Hahahahahahah." He clapped his wings and stamped his claws. "Hohohohohohohohoho. Wonderful. Wonderful."

He would have gone on laughing had not one of the rats startled us with a loud squeak. We looked the way the rat's stiff, crouching body pointed, westwards, down the floating river to White Horse Hill. There was nothing there but mist and glittering reflections off the frost.

"It's all right, it's all right," cawed the White Rook soothingly, running his wing over the back of the rat. He swivelled one eye on Pickles and Ben.

"Wonderful, wonderful . . ." He was cut short by a loud whimpering from two of the rats.

They were both looking down the floating river with stiff backs and tails.

We all looked down the floating river.

"Are you trying to frighten us?" said the White Rook to the two rats. He pointed one wing down the track but continued to look severely at them. "There's nothing there, all right? It's your imagination." He pointed a wing to the side of his head.

The third rat squeaked horribly and dived into the long grass. He was quickly followed by Ben. Pickles sat stone and within moments it was hard to tell where he was sitting, for instead of his clear stripy coat, broad back and brow, a grass hummock had appeared, streaky coloured with mist flowing around its base.

The White Rook hugged the ground but did not sit stone. He looked down the floating river. Then something jumped from the mist, a long dark shape, with a long tail, too distant to see properly. It vanished again, but there was no doubt it was running madly in our direction. The White Rook flew to the top of the hedge. I hid behind a grass clump.

Then suddenly, out of the mist, jumped the dark shape with the long tail, no longer in the middle of the track, but running fast on our side. It did not keep a straight course, but twisted sharply back into the middle as if to confuse a pursuer. It jumped again and it whined as it landed badly in one of the ruts. It dragged itself clear. The scurryings and short deep pantings got louder. I could see it running just under the surface of the mist. It was a rat, a great big rat, twice as big as our own.

It was exhausted. I could see it clearly now. It had eyes that neither blinked nor wandered, but stared as if focused on the distant skyline. Though it limped badly, it did not seem to know its wounds, for it still soared out of the mist. It did not pause when it landed. It was wild with fear, with stretch marks across his face so I could see the white of his eyes.

There was an excited flapping among the branches. "It's Black Eye. It's Black Eye. The messenger that never came home. He's come back." The White Rook called his name but it was no use. The rat passed us panting heavily.

"*Black Eye. Black Eye.*"

The rat showed no sign of hearing but vanished leaping into the mist.

The White Rook landed with outstretched wings. "It's no use. We will only frighten him." He turned to the rats.

"I want one of you to get him back safely to Blowingstone Wood."

The rats, upset by the experience, needed no encouragement and fought between themselves as to who should go. The chosen one unloaded half his pouch, and slipped into the mist to shadow Black Eye up the floating river in the direction of the Four Ways.

Ben was puzzled. "Why did you let him go? He may have seen things."

"Yeeees he may have seen things," hissed the White Rook, "but he will never be able to tell us. He has the look of someone who has seen too much." He turned to me and Pickles, who had now reappeared.

"Did you see something odd about him?"

He turned to Ben, raising his voice. "Did you not see it too? Am I the only one?"

We stared blankly at each other.

"Cat got your tongues?" cawed the White Rook with feeling.

"His tongue," breathed Ben quietly, "he had no tongue."

"Yeeeeees. He had no tongue."

We left Ram's Hill in silence, our party now six.

*   *   *   *   *

I saw the face of the White Rook's messenger all along the
hedgerows that reappeared briefly beyond the hill. I think it
preocupied Ben too, for twice he asked me to repeat my
description of the poor rat. It was certainly no ordinary fear
that had drawn those furfolds so deeply. I shuddered just to
think about it. It was not the sort you see in a cornered rat,
which goes when the threat passes—this had marked his
face like a hard frost on a window.

There were no hedgerows to shelter us now. Ben shuffled
double quick to keep up with the others. Pickles kept close
to the side, clearing easily with long strides the grass clumps
that proved such obstacles for Ben, as well as the rats weighed down with provisions. Sometimes the mist flowed over
the sides and for short stretches we could see the track
before us, the deep ruts of the cartwheels, the long grass at
the sides, giving way nearer the middle to coarser ratstails,
pineapple weed and the stars of woolly thistle. We hardly
saw Britchcombe Wood, so prominent from the Four Ways,
for it receded like a bald head from our vantage, hidden by
the contours of the slopes. Sheep pastures lay above and
below us, but we saw no sheep. There were solitary thorns
at field corners but no birds singing. There were vole tunnels in the grass but we heard no voles. There was furze on
the steep banks but no yellow blossoms.

"The sleeping and the dead, how alike they are," once
said the poet. The sun was in the west and in our faces. The
Ridgeway fell like a snake before us, taking the line of least
resistance, bending with the hills and shelving gently with
the slopes. There was still enough frost to glisten the branches but the grass no longer crunched beneath us. We took
it in turns to search the sky but we might as well have
searched the mist. Silence had becalmed the land. Nothing
moved except ourselves and the floating river moving
against us, and the sun slipping over the distant pines, a
smoky blue outcrop on the far ridge. A red light now crept
upstream.

The White Rook had taken the lead, keeping to the

110

bottom of a rut for speed, half-flying over obstacles as he surfaced briefly before sinking back into the mist. I could hear Pickles yawning ahead of me and the irritable rattle of Ben's claws as he struggled over some hidden stone, or round a woolly thistle. Our nerves were not the only thing on edge. There had been so much mist we hadn't noticed that the track had slipped closer to the edge of the steep slopes enclosing the valley beyond Britchcombe Wood. We were crawling on a knife-edge, and in places the heavy mist swirled over the side, filling the spaces, so it was hard to know where the land started and the sky began.

To dazzle our senses even more, the red light of the dying sun smoothed the brows of the hills, colouring the hedgerows and the floating river with its light. The pines were dark with red edges.

"It's beautiful," I told the others as we rested on a bank. "Just beautiful."

No-one took any notice of me or the sunset.

"How much farther?" groaned Pickles who was stretched on the grass.

"I agree," squeaked Ben.

"And so do I," said a rat in a fainter squeak.

"All right, all right," said the White Rook gruffly. He turned with dignity from exploring the sky and the distant ridges. He swivelled his eyes on us.

"Tired are we?"

"Yes," grunted Pickles. "I have missed my afternoon sleep, you realise." He yawned loudly.

Ben yawned too and so did a rat.

The White Rook peered into the sunset shielding his eyes with a wing. His feathers glowed with a crimson light. He grabbed some grass with his beak and pulled himself higher up the bank. His wing pointed a little north of the track to where part of the great mound of Uffington Castle, as high as a house, could be seen. He looked back at the sun which had slipped below the skyline. "The owlight is bad for travelling. Too many hungry eyes. We must be careful." He pointed again to the mound. "There, over there, past the first ridge and through the hollow is a place where we can sleep, under a thorn tree where a queen bee lives.

"Don't worry," he said, stooping below his wings to laugh at our anxious faces, "she's sleeping now."

There are not many queen bees on Uffington Castle and I cannot recommend looking for their homes by night. We searched up the ramparts and down the ramparts, across the ramparts and back again. We travelled halfway round the great plateau without any success, and it was only on our way back, when we gave up any idea of finding the queen bee, that Pickles found our nest for the night. It was a disused badger's run between two thorns and close to the edge of White Horse Hill. When we were all settled inside, it was way past star time, the sky above full of those pinpricks in the floor of heaven.

Chapter Ten

"What a beastly hole this is," cawed the White Rook. He was hunched under his wings, squashed between Pickles and a large root which twisted under his neck, pushing his beak up at a forty-five degree angle.

"We gave up too easily."

No-one listened to him.

He twisted his neck to get comfortable. "This is really very very inconvenient. A rook of my age too. Do you know how old I am?"

No-one wanted to know.

"Well I won't tell you." He sulked and muttered to himself. "I shouldn't have to ferret about in wretched holes like this."

We were in a tunnel which led nowhere for the roof had collapsed, leaving a space just large enough for us if we huddled together. We were out of the cold but through the entrance we could see the stars and the frost forming on the grass. There was no mist outside for it all flowed by gravity into the deep valley called The Manger tucked into the side of White Horse Hill.

"And I have a nasty feeling," continued the White Rook gloomily, "I should never have trusted that squirrel with all my berries. I knew he was out to cheat me. Oh dear. Oh dear."

"Will you be quiet?" grunted Pickles beside him, without opening his eyes. He rolled over onto his other side pushing Ben, who was curled at the end of his tail, hard against a chalk outcrop. He squeaked irritably, and fidgeted before settling down again. A rat was fast asleep by Ben with his mouth open, so that every time he breathed, and he breathed rapidly, the air whistled through his teeth and hummed on his whiskers, before being sucked back with short gurgling sounds. I was sitting by the tunnel entrance with my head on my knees. I was in a fitful sleep.

In my dream I was on a small hill. I could see a great distance with a skyline every way I turned. I did not recognise the land for there was no green or living thing that I could see. It was grey and jagged and instead of trees there were flames leaping from the ground, and black boulders of every size. I was with other children on the hill. We were holding hands and holding the hands of a lady dressed in green. She had long yellow hair. We were looking at something. One of the children pointed to something on the horizon. We all looked that way. There was something coming. I saw a brightness between the sky and the land. I saw dust rising. It was a long way off and moving at great speed. One of the children listened to the small hill. We all listened to the hill. There was a sound beating. "Who heard this?" said the lady. "A little child heard this."

I woke at that moment. The tunnel entrance was full of thin moonlight and the whistles, *zzzezes* of sleeping bodies. I had a cramp in my back and sleepy dust in my eyes. It was a while before I noticed that Ben was not curled by Pickles' tail. He had gone. He was not in the hole, I was sure of that. I saw a track through the grass where the frost had been rubbed away. It did not zig-zag but went straight until it disappeared down the far slope. I decided to follow.

I left quietly without waking the others and followed the track under the brightest night sky I had ever known. I came to the edge of the hill. I was on top of the world. The view was as big as my sleeping eye. I felt I could touch the stars if I had a ladder. I looked at the moon, as big and round as a farmhouse Cheddar. I looked down the hill, but not into the mist which covered the lower slopes and reached the farthest corners of the Vale; I looked at the great white horse galloping in the turf below me, frozen in that wild, ecstatic moment, as it has always been, down the centuries. Its broad white lines snaked across the slopes, charging down the steep broadside of The Manger with its eye, its single eye, fixed on the distant stars.

I stopped at the eye and looked again. I thought I saw something move. I saw the frost trail and followed it until I arrived back at the White Horse eye. I could see it now. It was a dark, pointed shape rocking on its hind claws and gazing towards the east where the sky blushed with the first hint of orange.

I ran down the slope forgetting the frosty edges of the grass. I jumped over the flints and would have cartwheeled had I been sure of keeping my balance. I was warm inside and I was in a hurry. I slid the last few feet and landed with two feet on the hard chalk back of the horse where it dipped below the rising mane. I would have run up the mane but instead I went as quietly as I could. Ben did not turn round when I reached the outer ring of the eye. His pointed snout pointed east, and he was still rocking in the eye, a circle of chalk as wide as a barn owl's wingspan.

I joined him but he did not look round. He sightwhiskered the distant landfall, past the slopes of sliding mist, the black edges of the woods and the darker hollows of the valleys still in moonshadow. There were orange patches in the east.

We watched together as the orange ran along the skyline streaking into bright red lights which flashed over the mist in the Vale. I rocked, too, with Ben, who now hummed to himself. The red light flashed more deeply and brilliantly, reaching farther into the Vale, catching the tree tops like flames, and throwing deep shadows around them. The yellow followed the red, and then the honey and the gold light.

Ben stood in the centre of the eye, still humming and sightwhiskering the approaching dawn. There were almost words in his humming, and, when behind us we heard a single, clear wind-hovering note, Ben shuffled slowly clockwise round the eye. One of the rats appeared on the edge of the mane playing on a pipe of cow parsley, a thin, threadbare music. It was then I heard his voice:

> I heard my name on a starry night
> O won't you come
> I was dancing in the pale moonlight
> O won't you come
> I was dancing round the White Horse eye
> O won't you come
> Yes go three times is to call your name
> O won't you come

The voices trebled. The White Rook and Pickles appeared close to the rat at the edge of the horse's mane. Pickles banged two snail shells together, slowly and in time to the tune. The White Rook blew through his feathers, a steady

humming buzzing sound. He flew into the eye, and walked with dignity behind Ben, singing with clear, raucous notes:

> O won't you come when the moon is right
> O won't you come
> O won't you come on the darkest night
> O won't you come
> O won't you come when you're far away
> O won't you come
> O won't you come at the break of day
> O won't you come

Pickles lumbered down the mane and into the eye. He joined the procession behind the White Rook and his voice added to the swelling sound that rocked us into dance on White Horse Hill.

> I wish I had feathers and I'd fly away
> O won't you come
> I'd fly to the east and west each day
> O won't you come
> I'd sing in the trees on a summer's night
> O won't you come
> And bury my head in the pale moonlight
> O won't you come

Then the rat scurried down and joined the end of the procession, singing:

> Owl is master of a starry night
> O won't you come
> It's better to hide when the moon is bright
> O won't you come
> I wish I could think of something to sing
> O won't you come
> But the song I sing has no ending
> O won't you come.

Then last of all, on the final turn round the eye, I joined the company and sang:

> I heard a voice in a hole in the ground
> O won't you come
> It had no words and the strangest sounds
> O won't you come
> I heard it when I saw the sun rise
> O won't you come
> On White Horse Hill at the break of day
> O won't you come

We broke into the loudest dawn chorus.

> *Springtime is coming in*
> *O won't you stay*
> *Springtime is coming in*

O won't you stay
O won't you stay

It was Pickles who spotted it as we climbed back up the steep slope; he had turned to take a last look of the Vale when he crouched suddenly. We all crouched. He pointed down the slope, past the winding sheep trails and into the sky towards Woolstone. We all saw it. A black shape skimmed lightly over the mist. It was flying across the cloud in The Manger. It was a bat, a greater horseshoe bat.

Chapter Eleven

When the sun rose on White Horse Hill we were far away on a sheep track skirting the shoulders of Uffington Castle. The five of us travelled single file with the White Rook leading. We travelled in the cold shadow of the ramparts, a giant ridge above us that circled the high plateau. We stayed in the hollow between the ramparts, following the places where the mist ran deepest, so we could hide at the slightest warning. The White Rook stopped when we approached a gap in the ramparts. He flew ahead and disappeared round the corner. He reappeared beckoning us with his wing.

"There," he cawed excitedly, "that's where we're going."

For the first time we could see the Vale, together with the Downland crest, and the endless stretching uplands of the interior. Everywhere we looked there were dark criss-cross lines of hedgerows cutting firmly through the mist, linking the beech hangers crawling on the skyline like giant hedgehogs. The mist rolled down the slopes exposing the choppy grasslands, but it clung to the level ground, not thickly as before, more like a thin veil hovering over the surface.

The White Rook pointed to the bottom of the slope, past the waves of frosted grass hummocks and to the twin hedgerows travelling west as the meadow pipit flies, up and down, up and down, to a ring of old beech trees in the west. They crowned a great wedge of turf with stones sticking from the sides.

"Thaaat," he said, "is Wayland's Smithy, not a place to

get blown to on a stormy night.''

"Nor on a still, clear day,'' added Pickles with a shiver.

I felt like shivering too. I heard the White Rook say he would not go near there for all the earwigs in oxeye meadow; I was affected by the greyness I saw everywhere, in the trees, in the hedgerows and in my thoughts. There was no wind to freshen our faces; there was no green thing to calm the eye or familiar smells to comfort us. The land was deserted as the sky, locked hard by the frost, and the skin of drifting mist.

Pickles interrupted my thoughts.

"Can you smell it?'' he asked, snorting deeply.

I spluttered as the cold air caught the back of my throat. I breathed again, this time more slowly, holding the air before breathing out. There was a hint of the smell you find under rotting bark, but nothing else.

The White Rook searched the cloudless sky, the distant trees and the dusty brown grasslands.

Ben sightwhiskered the great space without comment and so did the rats.

"The starlings,'' said the White Rook, "there's no sign of them anywhere. No sign of nothing.''

"And the smell,'' continued Pickles in a trembling

voice. "Where are the smells, the sweet pines and beech mast, the running mice, the musty sheep, the poohy fox, the grass, the sweet primrose? Where, where are they? There is nothing left."

"Except one," said Ben so clearly and softly, we all turned to listen. He sightwhiskered the empty sky. "The smell," he said, "it is the smell of the dead."

We did not linger in the gap, but followed the determined stride of the White Rook into the grasslands. We stayed close to the grass hummocks as there was no mist to hide us now. It had flowed to the bottom of the slope and filled the sunken route of the Ridgeway to overflowing. For a reason I cannot remember, Ben lagged behind, much to the annoyance of the White Rook. He ordered us to stop to wait for the master detective. He was some distance behind, so we rested while he shuffled forwards, stopping every so often as is his habit, to sightwhisker and continue if all was clear. He had lingered longer than usual after sightwhiskering a wide arc of the sky. We watched as he turned round a full circle, nearly tripping over a stone. He was looking to the south, and the ridge upon ridge of the never-ending uplands. The White Rook was on the point of cawing angrily when something strange happened.

We watched the silver streaking Ben's dark fur, blurring his pointed outline so he seemed to be made up of frosty grass, bits of stone and the odd patch of mist.

"Jumping spiders," squawked the White Rook, "that's all we need. What a time to take a nap."

He turned to face us and I watched the astonishment ruffle his tail feathers when only half of Pickles could be seen, and even that was fast turning into a frozen hummock. I took a little longer as I was not so experienced at sitting stone. I became little flints with frost glistening on me. The colour drained from the White Rook and he turned into a rabbit hole. As for the rats, they bolted for the safety of the longer grass farther down the slope. I watched them weaving their way through the hummocks.

We never saw them again.

None of us moved, for on the skyline of the interior something else was moving. It looked like a dark rain cloud from a distance, sombre-coloured and packed tightly as a thrush's nest. It skimmed along the horizon casting an ever increasing shadow. There was no wind but the cloud had wings of its own. It came as straight as an arrow, changing shape, so it was no longer round, but edge-on like enormous outstretched wings. It was a spectacle of ever-changing darkness, one moment flashing low over the land as a sparrowhawk hunts its prey, the next, soaring to hover in the sky. It hung there, somewhere above the twin hedgerows of the Ridgeway. I watched it burst four ways filling the sky with starlings. I could see chequered points of light in a thousand places. They joined and changed as easily as water in rapids; a mushroom shape with power to shelve one way and then another, to contract into darkness, expand into lightness. I heard rushings, wing upon wing upon wing beating; I heard the distant thunder and the church bells ringing, and there were shots and screams, not one, but the cries of a thousand ringing in my ears. The cloud, the bird, the starlings swooped into the grasslands below us. I closed my eyes, but I saw hunger that could never be filled.

I watched in heartbeat silence. The birds still quartered the grasslands, hanging in the air before dropping like stones to rise on an explosion of wingbeat, roving farther and farther into the Vale until the darkness passed from my sight.

* * * * *

I was trembling so much that the fear broke my concentration, and I returned to normal as far as my waist. I had no doubt that sitting stone had saved me. But from what? I could not stop shivering and thought I was being silly until I saw my companions were shivering too. They were appearing before me, throwing off more and more of their icy disguises. Ben rejoined us. We looked around, trembling and keeping our distance. We must have looked a pitiful sight, for seeing this we forgot ourselves and dashed into each other's arms, claws and wings to hug and be hugged for the joy of still being alive.

It took us a long time to settle down, especially as sitting stone on frosty hillsides is not a warm pastime. I was a winter newt disturbed from its sleep, only my eyes moving freely; the rest of me was still with the frozen earth. The White Rook's wings sparkled with pinpricks of light, and there were threads of frost on both Pickles' and Ben's whiskers. Ben thumped his tail to get warm, and when Burley snorted to clear his nose his breath rose like hot air balloons. The White Rook clapped his wings together, stamping alternately each of his claws.

"Dear oh dear," he hissed sadly, "this is just the end." He swivelled one eye on me. "Well you're not going to catch a weasel asleep like that."

I tried to say something intelligent but my tongue would not move.

He looked not unkindly at me. "What you need is a little south wind. Pickles. Come here." Pickles appeared and blew a stream of hot-air balloons at me until I was covered with misty breath. My body ached with the renewed sensation.

We were too exhausted to talk. We all did different things to wake up and keep the circulation going, but inside were the same thoughts, the same fears.

The White Rook hopped in front of us, his eyes bright against the blue sky. "Yeeeeees they're out to get us all right."

"The starlings?" I interrupted.

"Starlings," he hissed shaking his head so his beak rattled. "You shouldn't eat so many rose hips. It's bad for your eyes. There were no starlings . . . " His beak chattered with the effort to speak: "It was a great eagle with yellow eyes, hungry to fill its belly."

"No, no, no," burst in Ben. "It wasn't an eagle. It was a mad fox looking for me."

"Impossible," gasped Pickles with knitted furbrows. "Didn't you see it was a terrible swarm of hornets."

We looked at each other in amazement. Ben sat to recover his breath and he was so astonished I could see his pink teeth in his gaping mouth. He took from his pouch a black thing the size of an acorn, and swallowed it in two bites.

"How I hate hornets," moaned Pickles scratching his fur madly. He kept looking over his shoulder. "Do you think

124

they'll come back?''

The White Rook's eyes flashed. ''But it was an eagle I tell you. Haven't you got eyebrains? A cross-eyed eagle, just like the one mother rook used to tell of, the one with the sharp claws, the one that carries away the nasty rooks.''

Ben appeared to be dozing on the grass but I knew he was not-thinking. Suddenly he sprang, waving two claws and jumping up and down as if walking on hot coals.

''Do marigolds skip at night?'' he squeaked.

We watched him. He was dancing wildly in and out of the hummocks.

''Do butterflies eat jam tarts?''

He didn't wait for an answer. He hopped and skipped on two claws. He kicked the frost off the grass. He dived over bumps of chalk. He cartwheeled around us.

''What do snowflakes sing?'' He slid down the frosty side of a hummock. He tripped over a flint at the bottom and landed with a thud on his backside. He pushed himself upright.

''I've got it, I've got it,'' he squeaked.

''Does it hurt?'' said the White Rook.

''No, no,'' said Ben, dancing on his claws.

''How can you be so excited,'' groaned Pickles, ''when we have just been attacked by hornets.'' The mention of them made him scratch his back again.

''Can't you see?'' said Ben. ''They weren't starlings, or hornets, or eagles or mad foxes. *They*, or what we saw, were our deepest fears. The spider black shadow on the far side of the hill. The dead, the dying, all that is without life. All that is hungry for the living.''

''Do you mean,'' said Pickles cautiously, ''they weren't really hornets?''

''Yes,'' said Ben.

''What a relief,'' sighed Pickles. A worried furbrow crossed his face. ''But if they aren't hornets what are they?''

''Thaaaaat,'' hissed the White Rook, ''is what we are here to find out.''

Chapter Twelve

The starlings are the bogeys
and they all fall down
we shoot them in the trees and dig them in the ground
they're good for corn and barley
peas and turnips too
but never turn your back
for they're out to get you

The ruthless jingle of the boys and catapults, the crowds of villagers with their guns, haunted me as we ventured farther into the grasslands. We scrambled from grass clump to grass clump, but I did not see my companions, I saw only the worried face of my father and his brown peaked cap he wore when hunting. I heard fragments of conversation. I heard *"SHOOT SHOOT."* A storm of wings beating. A cry to beat down any heart. I heard *"SHOOT SHOOT."* I saw the blood on the trees, I saw red on my father's face. I heard nothing. *"HOORAY HOORAY!"* I heard the jingle again.

"Will you get down," said the angry voice.

I crawled between two hummocks.

"We'll end up as sitting pie because of you."

It was quiet among the hummocks. There was no mist to conceal us or waving grasses to break our shadow. We were about halfway down the grasslands with the White Rook leading. I must have strayed from the single file for they all gave me stern looks, including Ben.

The White Rook searched the sky and pointed with a flick

of his beak to a dark hedgerow snaking along the bottom of the slope. It was the Ridgeway. We continued single file, travelling at a mole's pace, which is another way of saying we travelled as fast as a hurrying bank vole. Our nerves were strained for the grazing lands were no place to linger. Once in the Ridgeway, we could hide and travel up the river floating between the twin lines of thorn.

We reached the twisted thornshade shortly before midday when the sun had started to swing westwards, and was high enough to catch the mist with brilliant points of light. We rested in the bank of moss and root, and old leaves. We were higher than the level of the mist, for horses, carriages and time had worn the trackway several feet below the fields on either side. We were too tired to eat heartily, instead we picked at our provisions, finishing off the dried worms, beech nuts and crystallised birch sap. Though no-one seemed concerned, I noticed there was only enough food for one more day.

After eating, we sank into the shadows, among the moss and leaves, and into a sort of forgetfulness. But none of us could sleep. We were listening too hard with one eye open, and when we caught each other's eye we shut them; but it was too late, we had recognised the fear in each of us. We stretched to get comfortable or curled into autumn leaves, all without success. Once Pickles turned over too quickly and rolled over the bank into the mist. He made so much noise trying to get back up, and spilled so much mist over the bank, we thought our worst fears had come true and the mist was about to eat us.

"Oh dear," said Pickles, "we'll never get to sleep here."

And just at that moment, as if he shouldn't have said it, we heard the grass rustling far above us, but there was no wind. We left our beds of moss, hardly daring to breathe, and crawled down backwards, sinking slowly into the mist. We watched the northern skyline, where the frozen grass ended. We heard the wind over the hill. We saw a black line spill above the horizon, growing larger as if it was the edge of a great shadow. I heard a storm of wings.

"The eagle, the eagle," hissed the White Rook.

I felt the dryness squeezing my throat and the shudder in my stomach.

"Don't look, don't look," cried Ben. "Get under the mist."

I dived into the bottom of the mist and lay in the largest of the ruts. I did not need to open my eyes to feel the ink blot spill across the sun. The light went out and it was darker still in the mist. Something flapped and hovered loudly above us, as if quartering the field of many hummocks and the twin hedgerows. The darkness passed and the steady wingbeat faded away down the track. The light returned. We lay in the ruts with our eyes closed.

"Listen," squeaked Ben by my side.

The sound returned. The storm of wingbeats approached this time more slowly. It hovered above us and I could feel the wind swirling the mist over my back. I could feel something searching the roots and the moss. I was too frightened to sit stone, though beside me, where Ben had been, was a small root with moss on it. There was too much mist for it to blow away. The wings flapped and hovered loudly, then, little by little, the sound faded, the mist settled and silence returned to the Ridgeway.

It, whatever it was, had passed away, but not the thought that now we would never be alone.

*   *   *   *   *

"Curse them," whispered the White Rook reading our thoughts, "they know we are here."

"How?" said Pickles. "I don't understand how." A deep trough divided his eyebrows, and his white-tipped ears trembled. "The bat, that bat. Of course, it must have seen us."

"Don't be so thistle-brained," said the White Rook. "What's a bat anyway?"

No-one spoke. We were back on the bank, under the thorns and between the mist and the grazing lands.

"What are we going to do?" said Pickles breaking the silence. "If we carry on like this we will make the biggest sparrow pie ever seen."

"He's right," said Ben.

"If we go back now we might still laugh and grow fat. Otherwise the lich-owls will find us one night . . . in a bloody pile."

The White Rook swivelled his eyes on a faint round disc far away in the sky. It was the rising full moon. He swivelled his eyes on us, the sunlight sparkling the frost on his hunched wings.

"Yeeeees Pickles is right. To travel by day is madness . . ."

"At last," said Pickles, heaving a sigh.

". . . but to travel by night is perfectly safe."

Pickles looked at Ben.

Ben stood on his hind claws and sightwhiskered the sea of grass, spreading far away to the west. He looked at Pickles.

"I'm sorry," he said, "I can't go back now. We have come too far." He pointed to the beech hangers in the distance." Somewhere, I know, somewhere out there we shall find our answer, among the deepest holes, down the farthest hedgerows, on the tops of the tallest trees. It's out there. We must find it. We must go on."

"Steady, steady," said the White Rook soothingly, "it's only a story."

Ben gritted his whiskers.

There was a long silence as if our thoughts weighed our tongues so we could not speak. The White Rook looked at Pickles.

"Talking of stories, I am reminded of a little one myself." He paused to get our attention then continued.

"I was just a young rooker at the time, fresh from the nest and had finished my schooling at the tallest elm in the district. Only the best went there and I was top of the class. I could soar for three breaths without flapping, catch butterflies on the wing, fly upside down if it rained and backwards to impress the others. Obviously with such an intelligent rooker and full of eyebrains as I was, I was top of the pecking order for my year. The others hated me for it. They said I had a funny colour so there must be something funny about me. I didn't listen to the rumours until it was too late. Five bully rooks from the second year experimented with me to see if I could fly with straw tied round my wings. I fell like a flying pig from the top of the tree and I saved myself from hopping the twig by landing in a cowpie.''

''How awful,'' squeaked Ben.

''It was, it was,'' said the White Rook. ''I lay there watching the dung flies and feeling very sorry for myself. I saw a daddy long legs crawl by and a little thing, the size of a dew sparkle, dash along the length of a grass blade, dive through the air, and land on the back of the big crawley's head. No matter what the crawley did it couldn't shake off the wolf spider. It lurched backwards and forwards, kicked its back legs up, swung to the side, brushed against the grasses but still the little spider stayed in its saddle behind its head. Suddenly, the dew sparkle scurried down a leg of the crawley, and onto a grass blade where it whipped a silken thread around the top, before leaping back onto the crawley's legs and dashing up the leg and into his saddle. The crawley kicked harder and charged into the grass, hoping to throw the rider. But it hung on, and, just as suddenly, ran down another leg, tied another grass blade and dashed back up to its saddle. The spider did this several times, each time down different legs, until there were so many threads, the big crawley could not move. The spider did not move but stayed in its saddle waiting for the daddy long legs to drop from exhaustion.

''And that,'' said the White Rook with emphasis, ''is what it did. After that I was never afraid to be small or alone for I knew it's all in 'ere.'' His wing pointed to the side of his head.

''See?''

''How could I ever have doubted it?'' said Pickles, stuttering with feeling. ''I will go with you where no rook has been before. I will go where moles fear to tread. I am ready for the longest tunnel.''

''This is getting out of hand,'' said the White Rook under his breath. ''No, no,'' he said to Pickles, ''we'll just go farther down the track and find a nice grass pillow.''

And that is what we did. The White Rook led us back into the floating river, and we travelled single file keeping to the centre rut where the mist flowed deepest. I had lost all sense of time so I didn't know how far we travelled. We sank farther and farther into the mist as the Ridgeway carved a deeper course between the hedgerows. It was safer to crawl than walk, and the mist covered me as completely as it did the others. We left the deepest rut and crawled over the misty ratstails, through the long grass we could not see and into the side of the bank. We settled between the roots of an old thorn, curling into each other for warmth. The White Rook spread his wings over us and kept watch in the mist.

It is hard to sleep when you know it is still the daytime. Even Pickles had trouble and he likes nothing better than to sleep all day and most of the night. The trouble was, his nerves were as fragile as frosted grass; a touch was enough to break them. He twisted and turned, sometimes jerking his head at a sound he had imagined. The White Rook caw-ed soothing noises but it still did not work. I thought the White Rook was going off his rocker when I heard him talk-ing to himself. I say talking, but the more I listened, the more it sounded not like words but sounds which were soft and curiously warming. It helped Pickles who twisted less, and even I closed my eyes. I heard Ben snoring, and I went to sleep, as did the others, with the White Rook's lullaby in my ears.

> La la la la la la la la lal
>   la la la lal
> When the wind blows
> would you sing me this song
> when the wind blows
> I will sing you
> I will sing you
> I will sing you this song
>
> When the wind blows
> I can feel the leaves sing
> when the wind blows
> I can feel
> I can feel
> I can feel the leaves sing
>
> When the wind blows
> I can hear the trees move
> When the wind blows

I can hear
I can hear
I can hear the trees move
    lallalalal alalalala lalalal alal
       lalal lalal alal lala
        alalal lalal lala
          lal ala

When we woke we had a shock. We were curled in the roots of the thorn tree as before, with the wings of the White Rook spread over us, but now we could see it. The mist had gone, except from the deepest rut. It was owlight but there were no owls, only a huge shining moon. We could see it through the criss-crossed branches of the thorns above our heads which were covered with its silver light. I woke first and tapped Pickles on the side. He heaved and grunted, stretching his foreclaws still with his eyes shut. He punched Ben on the snout.

Ben shrieked and immediately covered his mouth with a claw as he remembered where he was. We looked around us in amazement. The mist had really gone. We could see the ruts in the track, and the long grass on the far side. There was no hedgerow to block the view. We all took a deep breath. We looked across a glimmering silver meadow over which towered great black trees. They were spread in a giant's circle around the meadow. There were stars sparkling in the deep night sky. We could see them through the trees. But it wasn't that we looked at. Before us, not one hundred yards into the meadow, circled by the crown of beeches, were three standing stones. They faced us, three blocks from the side of a hill glistening with moonlight. There was a darker hole, a passageway between two of them, and behind that the rising spreading mound of turf and smaller stones.

We were opposite Wayland's Smithy.

Chapter Thirteen

"It's not true," said the White Rook, staring with open eyes, that rolled on either side of his beak. He tried to hide behind the root. "It's a dream, a horrible dream." He shut his eyes and opened them again.

"Oh dear, oh dear, it's still there."

We all stayed close to the roots, uncertain what to do, that is except for Ben. He stood and wandered a little into the track. He sniffed several times and sightwhiskered the meadow and the Smithy with several turns of his head.

"I think we had better go," said the White Rook stepping out from the bank and looking anxiously around him.

"I agree," said Pickles.

"Yeeees. We've a long way to go and it's too late for sightseeing now." He walked bravely into the moonlight, followed closely by Pickles.

"Wait," squeaked Ben.

The White Rook and Pickles stopped. They half-turned to look back.

Ben had continued sightwhiskering the Smithy. His stumpy tail beat the ground, slowly at first but more urgently. "I can't be sure . . . but I've seen this before."

"What!" exclaimed the White Rook still keeping distance, "you've never been here."

"Oh yes I have," said Ben.

"Oh no you haven't."

"I have. I know I have."

"It's too late for this sort of thing," said the White Rook, his eyes popping in all directions. "We really must be going.''

Ben reluctantly turned away and crawled slowly towards Pickles.

I followed and stopped for one last look. It was true, there was something familiar about the view, the way the mound rose through the trees. I had never seen such a large moon

and it was right above the standing stones. I heard Pickles call me, but I could not pull myself away. There was something familiar, the pattern of it.

''I've got it, I've got it,'' I whispered as loudly as I dared. Ben shot back, the others slowly.

''We really will be sparrow pie soon,'' said Pickles.

I took the ivory carving from the pouch and held it so the lines were clear in the moonlight.

''See,'' I said, ''it's the Smithy on a full moon.''

I was right. It was the Smithy on a full moon.

Ben snatched it from my hand and ran his snout over the edges. He held it against his tiny eyes, and almost at once his tail beat the ground excitedly.

''It's true, it's true,'' was all he could say.

His claw rattled on the ivory square. ''If this is the outside, and it is, then this,'' he said pointing to a cross-like scratch, ''must be the inside, the scene of Wormhole's last case.''

''Oh no,'' said Pickles, seeing what was coming.

''Mercy me,'' cawed the White Rook, ''You don't mean

to say . . . you're not serious?"

"My mind is made up," said Ben calmly. His tail stopped beating the ground. His mind was made up.

"You're going to listen to the ravings of a human thing," continued the White Rook in a quavering voice, "to believe in a few rotten old scratches . . . on a rotten old piece of ivory . . . to risk turning us all into sparrow dumpling. What for?"

"I'm going in there," said Ben even more calmly. "I won't be talked out of it." He stood his ground firmly, still sightwhiskering the Smithy glowing in the moonlight.

"Oh no," said Pickles.

"Oh dear," said the White Rook.

"I'm coming too," I said. I joined Ben's side.

The White Rook and Pickles stared at each other. The White Rook walked towards Ben in slow, solemn strides. He ruffled his throat feathers and sank his head back into his wings, flicking his beak one way, then the other. "Ben of Thornshade, you are crazy."

"I agree," said Pickles.

"You are crazier than all the earwigs on Ram's Hill." He paused and looked back at Pickles. "But if you think you are the only crazy one here, you are mistaken. I am just as crazy as you."

"So am I," said Pickles, less sure of himself.

"And just to show how crazy I am, I am going to come with you."

"And," said Pickles, last of all, "so am I."

*   *   *   *   *

How can I describe the stillness of that night? It was with us when we sheltered by the thorn roots; it was our companion when we crossed the track and into the silver grass of the meadow; we breathed it in when Ben stopped to sightwhisker; it lay with us as we crouched to search once more the stars in the night sky, and the glistening branches of the beeches.

We could see it clearly now. The great pile of ancient stones buried in the turf, caught in the moonlight, shining through the trees as arc lamps might light up a cathedral. It

135

was as hoary as time itself. Low and strong, in touch with simples, it belonged to the earth and its mystery. Who thought it? Who built it? No-one knew. Creeping moss, whorled ferns, lichens, dead branches, grass clumps shone on its back and sides. And when we looked upwards we could see the stars through the black branches of the trees, and the round, full moon above the standing stones.

We rested by the edge of the meadow, not knowing where we were going or why, but bound to follow Ben on the trail of the last case of Wormhole the First. He sightwhiskered the sky and spoke to us without turning.

"Now you don't have to come. I just want to have a look round it, and then I'll come back and join you."

"Not likely," said Pickles behind me. "I'm not staying here by myself."

The White Rook silenced everyone with an outstretched wing. He spoke with dignity. "I brought you this far and so I will take you further. It is my duty to lead."

He walked gravely to the head of the party. "Single file and keep behind me."

We travelled slowly along a cow trail, picking our way over the frozen bumps, and keeping close together for safety.

"See," said the White Rook, recovering some of his spirit, "there's nothing to be frightened about."

"It's a bit quiet," said Pickles behind me, "it's a bit like a spider's lounge." He was right, there was not one sound, not one flitter-mouse, to distract our attention.

We were halfway into the silver meadow, close to the dark twisted trunks circling the Smithy, and the passageway between the standing stones. The White Rook did not falter but strode bravely onwards.

"The trees," whispered Pickles as loudly as he dared, "I have the strangest feeling they are watching us."

We looked at the trees. We looked at Pickles.

"Not far to go," said the White Rook soothingly, "then we can all have a rest."

We were nearer the Smithy than the track now. The White Rook walked a little faster and Ben had to shuffle double fast to keep up. Again we heard Pickles' voice.

"The trees," he said, "I saw something move."

We looked into the bare branches of the trees. We looked at Pickles.

"Stop trying to frighten us," said the White Rook not so soothingly. "I promise you can have a rest when we get there."

He strode a little faster and kept looking nervously over his shoulders.

"The trees, I tell you, they're moving."

"Will you be quiet," said the White Rook angrily. "Do you want everyone to know we are here?"

We stopped to let Pickles calm down. He was shivering and pointing to a tree at the side of the Smithy.

I noticed with surprise one or two leaves I had not seen before.

"Pull yourself together Pickles; can't you see you're imagining things?"

The White Rook strode a little faster. My heart beat a little quicker.

We passed single file between the towering darkness of

two trees. The entrance loomed larger and larger between the standing stones. There was something too forbidding about them to enter in one go, the way the turf tumbled over a massive stone lintel at the back of the entrance. We stopped between the trees and the Smithy, but not for long.

"The trees," cried Pickles, his voice squashed with feelings, "look at the trees."

We looked and followed the frantic flight of the White Rook rushing beak first between the darkness of the standing stones and into Wayland's Smithy.

For outside something stirred. The beeches had blossomed with leaves, hanging on all the branches. And even as we flung ourselves into the cave, we could hear them flapping and rustling in the still night air.

*   *   *   *   *

In our panic we fled down the vaulted entrance of the cave, brushing past the ferns and moss on the stone sides, until we reached the darkness of the back chamber. It was a dead end, and the White Rook, in his hurry to escape, flew into the rock, followed closely by Pickles and myself. By the time we disentangled ourselves from each other and the long fronds of ferns, and the echoes had faded to a small drumming in our ears, Ben arrived with the news. He panted heavily, and it was only when he took a deep breath and let it out slowly, that he said: "The leaves . . . they're alive."

No sooner had he spoken than we rushed to the back of the chamber where we pressed against each other and the wall, a stone slab. We stayed silent and hardly breathed wishing we were somewhere else.

We were in a tight corner.

"Oh no," said Pickles, "I can hear it." We all heard it.

There was the heavy silence of a pine wood, and as we listened we could hear the low murmurs and hummings, as if leaves were being blown in the wind and were rustling on the ground. The sound came in waves, hollow, whistling sounds that skimmed on the wind, coming from every direction it seemed, but going nowhere. The echoes flooded the cave, travelling up the entrance, bouncing faster and faster off the stone slabs, so the wispy sounds swirled above us round the horseshoe chamber.

We were under the capstone, looking out from darkness. We could see down the vaulted entrance and out into the bright moonlit meadow and the dark hedgerow skirting the starry heavens.

"D-d-d-do you think," stuttered Pickles, "they are night-flying hornets?"

"Of course not," said the White Rook, peering past the ferns clinging to the stones and into the meadow, "they're probably nothing more than . . ." He never finished.

"*Bats*," shrieked Ben, trying to bury himself under Pickles, who was trying to claw his way through a crack in the stones.

First in our ears we heard them, then with our eyes we saw them. They came into the meadow as the night falls. They were neither here nor there, black nor white, but a strangely changing shadow, dancing and falling, gliding and hovering, impossible to describe, impossible to forget. We watched in heartbeat silence as they massed over the silver meadow, the moonlight silvering their ever-changing shadows. The horror of the sight wound our hearts like a spring. They were bats and yet more than bats. We watched them play in the night sky, until they were so many the stars went out, and the silver on the meadow turned black. There was just darkness and our cries in the back chamber. The darkness got blacker and then we saw the light appear on one side of the sky, then a little bit more at the front of the meadow and in other places. There was a pattern taking shape before our eyes. We could still hear the bats rustling, but there was something else, almost like a growl, and the padding of claws on frozen grass.

Ben shivered by my side, clutching my hand with his claws.

The shape grew stronger.

The darkness got blacker and the light got brighter. We could see the shaggy legs bent at the middle and hear the angry switching tail; we could see the flat-nosed muzzle and the bare exposed teeth, and the high-boned jaws which click-ed in and out of place. The yellow eyes glinted low to the ground and there were large pointed ears turned in our

139

direction. The growls and jaw clickings echoed round the cave. The thing crouched and crawled nearer the entrance.

"Mercy me," said the White Rook.

"Oh no," moaned Pickles.

Ben shivered even more and so did I.

Its claws scratched the grass. It growled louder. It crept forward. It stood between the standing stones. It was preparing to spring.

"*Marigolds*," shrieked Ben, jumping up and pinching Pickles out of his stupor. "*Think Marigolds.*" He smacked the White Rook round his bald cheeks. "*Think Marigolds.*"

I could hear the padding of the beast. It was running down the entrance. It was between the vaulted stones. It sprang.

"*Marigolds*," cried Ben.

"*Aaaaaargh*," cried Pickles.

The beast stopped in mid-air; one moment we looked into its yellow eyes and growling teeth, the next it parted into several shapes. The colour drained from its face and body, and instead of a switching tail, leaves were flying and rustling in the cave entrance. The beast had vanished. There was a layer of leaves between the standing stones.

No-one moved. "Listen carefully," said Ben not taking his whiskers off the entrance, "think of nothing else but marigolds."

We all thought of marigolds, obeying without question the master detective.

Before our eyes something strange happened. There was a stirring in the leaves. A green shoot appeared, then two small leaves which got bigger as the shoot got higher. We watched in amazement. It was a marigold.

"Isn't that pretty?" said the White Rook trying to be reasonable.

"Yes it is," said Pickles trying to get a grip on himself.

The green shoot got bigger until it was nearly as high as the standing stone. The end swelled into a tight knot. It started to open.

"It's going to flower," said the White Rook.

The orange flower shone against the silver meadow and the starry night sky. It started to shrivel.

"It's dying," said Pickles.

The flower shrivelled into a crown of short straws. The green stem faded too and buckled over onto the entrance floor among the leaves.

"Well that was nice," said the White Rook, adding quickly, "I think we had better go." Pickles agreed. They got up and were about to go when the leaves stirred again.

Several green shoots had appeared. The leaves got bigger, branching out on all sides until they reached the top of the standing stones. Then they flowered, wilted and collapsed farther into the entrance. Almost immediately twice as many green shoots appeared, along with the leaves. There were so many they blocked out half the light. They flowered and seeded and fell farther into the cave.

I don't like the look of this," said Pickles. He turned to Ben who was scratching his whiskers.

"I'm getting tired of marigolds."

"I never liked them that much anyway," said the White Rook, "too much of a weed."

The marigolds filled the entire entrance by now, blocking out most of the light. They advanced towards us, multiplying faster and faster.

"I think we should not-think marigolds," said Ben when the plants were at the edge of thehorseshoe chamber.

It was a close thing. The colour drained from the marigolds just as they sprouted among us. The leaves fell from the flowers and were twice as deep as before.

"Wind. Think Wind," cried Ben.

No sooner had he said it than wind came from the cracks of the stones and rushed among the leaves, dashing them against the stones, past the hanging ferns and out into the moonlit meadow, where they changed into countless fluttering wings, vanishing from the entrance as smoke does from a chimney. We could see them hovering and gliding, skimming low over the silver meadow and the starry night sky.

"We've got to get out of here," squawked the White Rook, tapping the stones around us with his beak.

Pickles got on his hind legs and ran his paws along the ridge between the standing stones and the great capstone. Ben searched the corners of the chamber, sniffing and scratching every crevice.

"It's hopeless, it's hopeless," groaned Pickles flopping back onto the floor. "We're trapped, caught in a blind mare's nest." He stared through the darkness of the passageway and into the moonlit meadow. "That's the only way out."

"So much for your fears," said the White Rook looking at Ben. "Whatever's out there is alive . . . and **very** hungry."

Ben twittered excitedly. "Don't say that. It only has eyes when we give it eyes. It only grows when we let it grow. We're safe in here as long as we can not-think and keep awake until the dawn."

"How can you be so sure?" asked Pickles.

"Because when the dawn comes the bats sleep."

Even as he spoke we heard the countless fluttering of tiny wings, soaring over the meadow. The sky darkened as more and more of them swarmed before us, travelling in thin wispy trails like spiralling smoke patterns.

We sat in the back chamber, and on Ben's order tried to think of nothing. Ben dozed beside me, the White Rook and Pickles stared at the ceiling and I kept counting to seventy eight and counting it backwards. As long as we kept our minds empty, the fluttering wings still fluttered harmlessly outside. Twice I had to jog Pickles from snoring, for as soon as one of us fell asleep, the sky was drained of wings, and black haunting shapes appeared. They faded into a thousand pieces when we all concentrated. How long we kept this up I have no idea, but the strain of not-thinking and keeping awake slowly wore us down, so the black haunting shapes appeared more and more frequently. And each time they did, it was harder and harder to scatter them.

"This is hopeless," said the White Rook at last, "we must do something."

"There is nothing we can do," said Ben sightwhiskering his friend. "We have to sit this out and not-think."

"I can't sit here like a pudding waiting to be eaten. I've got to do something." He stared down the passage. "Look, there's nothing in the sky. They've gone. It's our chance to go."

No-one moved, except Pickles who rubbed his eyes.

It was true. There was nothing in the silver meadow, just the dark line of the Ridgeway at the bottom and the starry night sky.

"Just as I hoped," continued the White Rook. "If we can get back to the track there's enough mist in the deepest rut to hide us as we escape."

"I agree," said Pickles, "you have got to catch slugs while you can."

Ben agreed reluctantly, and only after sightwhiskering the meadow several times.

The White Rook led us single file up the passageway and stopped when he got between the two standing stones. We could see the ruts of the cow trail clearly across the meadow, and even the hole among the roots where we had slept. Now the moon had moved, the shadows of the trees fell at a slant in the direction we were going, stretching far across the meadow. The White Rook stepped into the grass and stepped back again.

"Did you see that?" he said.

"What?" said three anxious voices behind him.

The White Rook stepped into the grass again and stepped back. His tail feathers trembled but he still spoke with dignity.

"I don't know," he said. "But I thought I saw something move when I moved and go back when I went back."

He stepped into the grass and then stepped back quickly.

We all saw it now. One of the tree shadows had moved forwards with him and backwards, but just a little too slowly.

We looked at it carefully, though we could not see the tree for it was on the other side.

"It's very ragged for a tree trunk," said Pickles.

"And the branches are very thick," I said. "Which tree is it?"

We looked up at the stones. I saw the claws which gripped the side of the capstone, and the feathers thickening up the long legs, the mailcoat of feathers between the two outstretched ribbed wings with moonlight shining through them. There were bloodshot eyes set deeply over an ugly ripping beak.

In the eyes of the eagle was the hunger I had seen in the starlings, the hunger we had seen in the mad fox. The hunger of the dead for the living, the hunger that can never be filled. The eagle flapped its wings screeching three times.

KEEEEEEIEeee KEEEEEEIUEeee KEEEEEEIUEeee.

Everything happened very quickly. We fled back into the cave, fleeing from the White Rook's childhood phantom. We fled into the horseshoe chamber. The White Rook shivered in the corner snapping his beak. Ben dozed and snored in a state of not-think, while Pickles and I, despite the shuddering which shook our bodies, fought desperately to empty our minds. I was too exhausted to not-think so I clung wildly to an image of a custard pie.

There was a great flap and rush of wind as two enormous talons landed at the end of the passageway. It stooped so its body filled half the entrance of the cave. The stars sparkled above its wings crossed over its back. For a moment the bloodshot eyes turned yellow with crinkly edges. The eagle screamed twice, and powered by some unseen strength, squeezed into the passageway. Still it advanced, shaking off the crinkly edges and the yellow patches flickering on its beard of ragged throat feathers.

I could hear Pickles breathing heavily, the White Rook shaking in the corner, and the rhythmical snoring of Ben and the whistle which followed as he breathed out through his whiskers. I could feel the hot and dry breath of the bird now. It was halfway between us and the standing stones, struggling to move forwards. My thoughts weakened and the last of the crinkly edges faded from the bird's wings. It stood before us triumphant, ready to claim us into its timeless world.

I made a last stand; the one thing to make them forget themselves. "Grub's up," I said, my voice shaking.

"Food?" squeaked Ben, waking with a start.

"Did you say eats?" said Pickles and the White Rook together.

I opened my pouch and flung a handful of dried worms, nuts and silver birch sap before them. I could have cried with relief when they flung themselves on the food. I still thought wildly of a custard pie.

The fiery eyes of the eagle turned yellow and there were crinkly edges on his massive bill. He no longer advanced, but was hunched under great ribbed wings at the edge of the horseshoe chamber. Only I saw him, the others were too busy eating, for when they eat they can only think of one thing at a time.

I emptied the pouch and gave them all the food.

"Mmmmmmmm," sighed Ben, "nothing like dinner."

I knew we were safe as long as the food lasted. I thought of a custard pie.

The eagle's face had turned yellow and instead of wings there was pastry case lining.

"And look," said Pickles pointing to the edge of the horseshoe chamber, "custard pie for afters. My favourite."

They all eyed the custard pudding, except for me. For once I was grateful for their table manners. They fell on the custard pie, ripping it apart, and did not pause until every last crumb and every bit of custard had gone.

They returned to the back of the cave and flopped to the ground.

Ben looked at me, still licking his claws. "Not hungry?"

I said nothing.

"What's that?" said Pickles, pointing with his claw to the night sky. "Can you see it?"

We all looked.

"Bless my soul alive. It's a shooting star."

"So it is," cawed the White Rook. "Better have a wish."

"I wish, I wish," said Pickles. "I will soon be in bed."

They all yawned at the mention of sleep, and before you could say Jack-in-the-hedge the chamber echoed with the sounds of contented slumber.

* * * * *

I was in no mood for sleep. I had too many thoughts of our narrow escape. I sat propped against the wall for a long while half searching the shadows for half imaginable things. I don't know how long I sat there in that mood, willing my

145

eyes to stay open, but soon, and soon enough, I gave way to a deep sleep.

I was on the green hill I had seen before. I could see a long way on every side. I did not recognise the land for there was no green or living thing that I could see. It was grey and jagged and instead of trees there were flames leaping from the ground and black boulders of every size. There were other children on the green hill. We were holding hands and holding the hands of a lady. She had long yellow hair. One of the children pointed to the horizon. We all looked that way. There was something coming. I saw a brightness between the sky and the land. It was a long way off and moving at great speed. We watched holding hands, keeping close to the lady. It got brighter. It lit up the whole sky and where there were flames there were now trees, and earth where there had been rocks. The land rolled like a green wave behind the brightness and there were clouds rising where it met the flames. It rained and there were blue streams. ''Who saw this?'' a child asked the lady. ''A little child saw this,'' she said.

I woke thinking it was the dawn, but I could still see the stars in the night sky. There was a bright light in the horseshoe chamber, so bright it picked out the edges of the hanging ferns on the stones. I could see the shooting star Pickles had seen. It was bigger than all the stars put together. It was a long way off but getting brighter every moment. It flew across the heavens in great shafts of light, lighting up the cave as if it were the sun. I stood up. I shook Ben.

''What is it?'' he squeaked grumpily. He ran his claws through his whiskers then straightened with fright. He dived into the fast-vanishing shadows, waking Pickles and the White Rook.

''Lawks,'' cried the White Rook hugging the wall.

''Oh no,'' said Pickles shielding the light from his eyes.

It was too bright to look into the shooting star. I joined my companions in the shadow.

''This is it,'' said Ben gritting his whiskers. ''I am too tired to fight any more but I shall go with dignity.'' He squatted on his hindclaws, relaxing his whiskers so they fell evenly across his snout. I sat beside him.

We waited in silence. As the light grew fiercer we huddled closer together. We were packed in the corner between two stones. There was so much light the chamber seemed to hum. Pickles breathed so deeply his whiskers tickled my face. Ben sat serenely and the White Rook fidgeted with wild eyes, rocking to and fro.

With the first breath of wind, the leaves in the passageway flew into the air and shrivelled into nothing, little points sparkling like fireflies before vanishing into the brightness.

The White Rook stepped clear of the wall. "I will not sit here like a stuffed owl and go out with a whimper." He shook his beak. "No. I will go out bravely."

He scrambled over Pickles' side and hopped into the centre of the chamber. He shielded his eyes with one wing. He thumped his claw as if beating out a tune. His voice crackled into life.

> Oh happy the rook
> on the top of the tree
> he loves to go flying
> he loves to go flying

His voice faltered. He staggered on his claws still shielding the light with a wing.

Pickles suddenly moaned at the sight of his friend going under. He pushed himself from the ground. "No, no." He buried his head in his side and crawled into the brightness. He reached the White Rook's side. The White Rook collapsed across his broad back, still shielding his eyes, still singing, his voice swelled by the gruff tones of Pickles.

> He loves to go flying
> he loves to go flying
> across the green fields

Ben stood in the last of the shadows, and I followed him as he shuffled slowly into the light. Not even the wind-rush could drown our voices. At the end we had no cares. We sang with every last bit of ourselves, propped against each other, blind to the light that blinded us.

he loves to go flying
he loves to go flying
across the green fields
with a slug, slug slug slug
and a truffle or two
we'll sing this song
and hail the new moon

"The end. The end," cried the White Rook. "We're ready." He started to sing the song again but his voice was swallowed by the wind which rushed past and would have carried us into the stone wall had we not clung to each other as hard as we clung to the earth. The brightness hummed with a thousand notes. I heard streams roaring down a mountainside. Our minds were filled with brightness. I could see stars. I saw them glittering. I could hear it pounding across the night sky. I could see the colours of green and gold and red. They were its eyes. The wind was the path it made with its great white body. I could hear it galloping down through the heavens. I could feel its racing breath warming our bodies. There was no time to stop. There was no time. It was forever rushing and not moving. The shooting star fell to earth. I heard the cry of the night being extinguished by light. I heard the cry of the heavens calling for its children. I saw the trees ravaged by beetles; the dolls in the snares. The men marching to war. I felt the horror of the hunted. The black flutter of wings. "Death . . . Death . . . Death . . ." they screamed. The light. The light. I saw the faces of the hurrying people too busy to see their dying. I was at the door of the manger, the horseshoe chamber of Waylands. Not a grave, but a door, a passage between two worlds; a spirit cavern for the dead and all that is dying. Waiting, waiting for the *Sound*. The sound it makes on its long star haul to earth. Once in a big time it comes and now is the time.

I saw the shining white mane. It was too bright, too bright. The wind pulled at our bodies. There was no time. It was forever rushing and not moving. I could see the moonlight bridge. I could see it reining on a bridle of light, caught in mid-gallop, halting awhile as it always had done and always will. The light barely touched the earth. I heard the sound of the star breaking. The night finished here. I was at the door of the manger. I could see its blood-stained hooves. I heard them pounding between the standing stones. Calling the night, calling the dead and all the things which have ended. Calling them home, no longer free to wander, choke and haunt the living. The shooting star fell to earth, but not the light, the living light passing through the horseshoe chamber; that vanished, not into the night but into the huge unknown; speeding quickly across the heavens, in and out among the stars.

The night-mare had passed.

I heard the bells ringing in Wayland's Smithy. I heard the larks above White Horse Hill. I saw the flowers opening. I saw the barley growing. I saw the lambs in the meadows. I heard the earth singing. And even when the last of the light had faded to a pinprick in the sky, and the last of the stars had disappeared, I could still hear the song ringing in my ears.

> Green orange brown and grey
> are the colours I sing all the day
> they're the colours of me
> the colours of you
> the song of the seasons too
>
> Grey's where the colour rests
> where the song lies under my breast
> it's the time of the year
> when the life moves within
> it's when I build my own nest
>
> Green is there, if you look
> it grows from my earthly brown
> it's the life you can see
> it's the loving in me
> the light of a new spring day

Orange is my fiery breast
that rules my heart you'll see
it stands for the life that's revealed within
summer's own glory in me.

I'm a robin by now you have guessed
I'm the seasons where life is all blessed
if you see this in you
you'll see me there too
the song of the sky in the blue

Chapter Fourteen

The memories fade with old age. But not all. I still remember the last time I saw Ben. We were in his office at Thornshade, sitting opposite each other at the table. I watched him noisily and greedily devour a pile of freshly caught worms. He was talking to himself as he gulped down the worms.

"Eenie, meenie, along comes moley and down he go."

He did this until he had eaten the twenty worms.

I cannot describe the feelings I experienced then. I was a seed about to burst. A thundercloud about to rain. I was not myself, for I was feeling homesick, as restless as a spring bubbling from the ground. Ben must have sensed my thoughts for he sightwhiskered me carefully. He waited for me to speak.

"Ben," I said at last, "there is something troubling me."

"Yes."

"I'm not quite sure what it is, but it's troubling me." I paused. "I want a yes or a no."

"Yes or no," repeated Ben.

"Not yet. I want you to tell me honestly."

"Honestly," repeated Ben scratching his whiskers. "Sounds serious."

"Well it is and it isn't, but it's important for me to know."

He waited for me to speak.

"Tell me the truth . . . am I alive?"

"Oh dear," said Ben getting up suddenly. "I am going

to lose another apprentice.'' He turned to me. ''I wish you wouldn't ask me these questions.''

''I've got to,'' I said, ''for my own peace of mind. Am I alive?''

''Of course you are,'' he said slowly, too slowly for my liking.

''You hesitated.''

''No I didn't.''

''Am I alive?'' I said more firmly.

''Dear, oh dear, and apprentices are so hard to find too.'' He looked at me. ''Yes you are alive . . . Well, sort of.''

I did not like his answer. ''What do you mean sort of?''

He searched for the right words. ''Not quite alive . . . but close.''

Before I had time to think, he said, ''Are you well enough to travel . . . ? I know how tired you must be.''

I nodded.

''Follow me.''

I followed him through the door where I had heard him shouting at his servant. I followed him down the smooth-faced tunnel with the crystals glinting in the roof corners. I felt the same tell-tale draught tickling my face. I followed him down the winding ways until we reached a large airy chamber, where there was a pile of stones and roots, and where the light shone through the ground. I recognised the place where I had seen Ben digging, blunting his claws removing the earth and stones. They had gone now, along with the sarsen stone. I could see its old weathered lines on the green grass. The blue sky above.

''You are sure you are well enough?'' he said again.

''Of course I am.''

''Then close your eyes,'' he said, ''and think of something very, very special. Something that is the most precious thing in the whole world. If you do that you shall see what only little children see and little things in hedgrows never forget.''

''Are you ready?'' he asked.

I nodded.

''Farewell'' he said. ''And tell them that we love life too.''

Those were the last words I ever heard my friend Ben say.

I opened my eyes. The brightness! How it hurt. I could see swimming shapes. They would not stay still. There were sounds. I could not say what they were or where they came from. I saw daisies. They were climbing up something. I moved my head. How slowly it turned. I tried to touch it but my hand would not move. I turned my head the other way. The brightness! I saw blue sky. There was a tree. All green. I saw a boy in bed. His head was wrapped in bandages. I looked at him and he looked at me.

I knew then.

I saw the pot of flowering daffodils. The curtains. There were people in the room. I saw my family. They were looking at me. Some were crying. I heard my mother's voice and felt her hand.

"Thank God," she said, "baa lamb's woken up."

Peter Please has lived in the Thames Valley for most of his life, and worked as a journalist and editor until he left to write and earn a living as a gardener. *Chronicles* started life as a short story ten years ago, inspired by Peter's fascination with the legends surrounding the Uffington White Horse and his love for nature. Peter now lives in Bath with Caroline Waterlow, who drew the illustrations for *Chronicles*, and their young son Ben (pure coincidence?).